Jeff's Journey

Jeff's Journey

RICK HERRICK

RESOURCE *Publications* · Eugene, Oregon

JEFF'S JOURNEY

Resource Publications
An Imprint of Wipf and Stock Publishers
199 W. 8th Ave., Suite 3
Eugene, OR 97401

www.wipfandstock.com

PAPERBACK ISBN: 978-1-6667-0841-7
HARDCOVER ISBN: 978-1-6667-0842-4
EBOOK ISBN: 978-1-6667-0843-1

JUNE 2, 2021

To Jane and Paul

With Deep Gratitude

Contents

Acknowledgements

MANY FRIENDS HAVE HELPED with earlier drafts of the book or with information relevant to constructing the plot. These friends include: Carol and Stephen Humpherys, Sarah Moore, Jane Lawson, Cyndee Dennehy, and Mary Woodcock. My good friends Amy and Ken LaDeroute mentored this book. Ever since meeting them twenty-five years ago and hearing them sing, I have wanted to write a story about a singing duo. To all of you, many, many thanks.

Jane and Paul were parents of a son who never quite measured up. My mother's earliest dream was for me to become President. When I developed a keen interest in the Bible at an early age, she modified that dream to bishop in the Episcopal Church. Instead of going to seminary, I wrote *The Case Against Evangelical Christianity*. In the nineteen eighties, I became the editor of a counterculture magazine. On a trip to visit my parents during that time, my Dad, a lifelong Republican, said: "Rick, I can't give your magazine to any of my friends, but here's a check to help move it along."

Toward the end of her life, my mother fell from a deck and ended up in intensive care on a ventilator. She wanted to die and needed me to plead with the medical staff to take her off the machine which would allow that to happen. Because her doctors were convinced she would recover, I said no. When the respiratory therapist took her off the ventilator so she could briefly respond to me, she yelled out: "You have never, ever, done anything I wanted you to do." And then she smiled, reached for my hand, and continued: "But I love you madly."

That's how it went. I lived my own life; and in the eyes of my parents, at least as far as I was aware, I could do no wrong. Humans are not set up to love unconditionally; but, with me, my parents came close. It is therefore my greatest honor to dedicate this book to them.

Rick Herrick

Spring, 2021

Prologue

Rev. Jeffery T. Peterson
Trinity Church
81 Elm St.
Concord, MA 01742

The Rt. Reverend Frank M. Gilmore
The Episcopal Diocese of Massachusetts
138 Tremont St.
Boston, MA 02111
April 22, 1995

Dear Frank,

I am resigning as senior minister of Trinity Church effective immediately. I spoke with Charles Covington yesterday, and he is fully prepared to assume my duties until such time as you find a replacement. Rebecca will no longer speak to me, and will remain in Concord as our organist and Music Director. I am leaving Massachusetts tomorrow for the mountains of North Carolina.

Here's the bottom line on all of this. I gave a traditional Easter Sunday sermon two weeks ago, and I'm having a hard time living with myself. The story of Jesus as a salvation figure is a myth. There is no historical evidence to support these Christian claims. You know it, I know it, and most of the clergy in this diocese know it. I will no longer be a party to perpetuating this massive consumer fraud.

As you also know, Trinity Church is a successful church with many fine members. You should have no problem finding my replacement. While you and I have differed on many issues, I have always appreciated your "hands off" style of management. Although we were never golfing buddies, I can attest to the fact that you were a good boss.

I do have one favor to ask. Rebecca had no part in my decision; and, as I indicate above, wants to remain with the church. I hope you can help to make that happen. As you well know, she is a talented musician, and a hard worker with a total devotion to Trinity Church.

Best wishes for your continued success.

Sincerely yours,

Jeff Peterson

Chapter 1

New Beginnings

I RAN FROM MASSACHUSETTS and Trinity Church. There's a big part of me that would like to do it over again, not the leaving part but the abruptness of it all. I should have consulted with the bishop, said goodbye to my many friends both within the congregation and outside of it, and most importantly, I should have shared my misgivings about the church with Rebecca.

I didn't leave the church because I was burned out with my profession, a common problem within the ministry, but it was not my problem. I knew how to relax, and I had lots of friends outside of my congregation. I made it a point to spend time with them—mostly through sports. We played golf together in the summer and squash in the winter. The role of being a minister was not oppressive for me or my family as it is for some. Occasionally it was inconvenient in that it made casual friendships more difficult, but it wasn't oppressive. Role-playing is part of the job in any profession.

I also didn't leave the ministry because of the theological issues I mentioned in my letter to the bishop, although that was what I believed to be true during the immediate period surrounding my departure. As you will see, many of these issues have bothered me since attending seminary in the early seventies. I set a goal five years prior to leaving the church of slowly leading my congregation into the twenty-first century theologically. I had made some progress, but it wasn't easy going. Church members are uncomfortable dealing with intellectual issues, and they don't like change. I am a little disappointed now that I didn't provide more forthright leadership on these matters, and yet my life is finally going so well it is hard to imagine serving another mainline Protestant church.

Unfortunately, that last statement jumps far ahead in my story and certainly does not describe my situation in the spring of 1995. I left Concord then for the mountains of North Carolina to heal some rather deep psychological wounds. I have often thought that the male species is genetically programmed to be silent, to live alongside others, but to keep what matters most, our feelings, inside.

It has been my hunch that we men devised this strategy thousands of years ago to succeed at the hunt. Males wanted companionship, needed the protection of others, and yet success at the hunt required silence. Maybe not all men are predisposed in this way, but it describes my psychological profile well.

I am a silent one. It is a strategy that has served hunters well for thousands of years, but it is a disaster for one who has been psychologically hurt. And I should have known better. I had been a professional caregiver for almost a quarter of a century. My stupidity ate away at my marriage like Chinese water torture, slowly, steadily over several years, drip by drip, and finally my inner problems overwhelmed me at a time of crisis. It was like a tea bag left too long in steaming water. My mood became progressively darker, more toxic, bitter to the taste, until finally, in desperation, I fled from my marriage and profession.

I set off in April of 1995 for the mountains of North Carolina to heal and to look for answers. In pursuing such work, a good strategy for men who are prone to silence is to fish or to walk. The physical repetition of both activities helps to free the mind, to unclog it. My preference was for walking. In those first few months I was in Watauga County, I averaged forty miles a week. I hiked every trail I could locate within a fifty-mile radius of Boone.

On those solitary hikes, I revisited and relived the events that were related to and had become enmeshed within the deep layers of my psyche. It was a strategy I decided upon on the drive to Boone from Concord. I wanted to get my life back. The first twenty-one years had been so easy, carefree, storybook really, and I wanted the last third of my life to end that same way. My self-imposed therapeutic regime was difficult at first, quite painful at some points in my inner exploration, but I kept to it and eventually the thick black cloud that had encased my heart and poisoned my daily living began to lift.

I chose the mountains of North Carolina as my place of escape because of a trip Rebecca and I had taken in the early eighties. We had attended a professional conference in mid-July in Hendersonville, North Carolina, and afterwards we drove north, spending eight days in bed and breakfasts in Blowing Rock, Valle Crucis, and Linville.

Rebecca described these tiny mountain villages to friends back home as lovely and quaint while I believed I had found a new home. That's quite an admission for a lifelong Yankee, but it's an accurate description of how I felt both then and now. There was something about the lush greenery, wooded peaks, sparkling streams, diverse hardwoods, and tightly compacted valleys that dug into my soul.

Now that we're on Rebecca, let me be fair from the outset and report to you that she was not part of my problem. Sadly, she was not part of the solution, but she had no role in contributing to my deep sadness. In fact, we had a very successful professional marriage. As you learned from my resignation letter, she was the music director and organist for our church. She is an immensely talented musician and was very dedicated to her job. She also functioned, informally, as an associate pastor, making hospital visits and pastoral calls when my schedule made such work difficult. Often, when circumstances permitted, we would do this work together. Actually, we enjoyed doing this work together. I can't honestly remember ever fighting with her over matters of church business.

The church was her life, and it remains so to this day. As her minister and superior, she looked up to and respected me. Somehow, despite our demanding professional schedules, we managed to have two wonderful children: Brenda Anne Peterson, born January 21, 1971, and Scott Hansford Peterson, born September 7, 1973. Both Brenda and Scott were high school and college athletes, and Scott was active in high school theatre.

You often hear parents complain about living in the same house with teenage children. I know there can be problems, but there is nothing more exciting for a parent than to attend an extracurricular event in which their child is participating. Rebecca and I made a career out of rooting for our kids, which lasted for more than ten years.

Our problem was not the kids. It wasn't until after both were away at college that I began to sense there was trouble in our marriage. For the longest time I pretended not to need much in our relationship, but that was a mistake. I needed warmth and caring and a person with whom to be intimate. It wasn't only sexual intimacy, though that was part of it. The sad fact was we shared little between us that was important. When faced with a family crisis, it was soon evident, at least to me, there was nothing there. Such a crisis can work to bring two people together or it can drive them apart, placing them in separate orbits that rarely intersect. The latter outcome best describes our situation. I asked Rebecca to come to North Carolina with me, but she slammed the door in my face. In retrospect, I am glad she stayed. Our divorce became final on August 4, 1997.

*   *   *

"Sweetwater Lane," I mumbled as I glanced again at George Edwards' directions. "It should be someplace around here on the left." What a great address from which to send Christmas cards to my northern buddies, I thought grinning. After two weeks of motel living in Boone, hiking the trails along the Blue Ridge Parkway and exploring several tiny mountain villages, I was ready to find permanent housing.

One place I had overlooked in my travels was Bethel, a small community in the western section of Watauga County next to the Tennessee border. But I was on my way there now, and it was some trip. How the hell am I going to get any place in the winter? I thought to myself as I looked in the rearview mirror to see if there was anyone behind me. I did not want to be pressured on this narrow, winding mountain road. This was my third day of looking for rental property, and I was hoping it would be the last one.

Two miles later I found Sweetwater Lane, turned left, and entered a narrow gravel road that went straight up the mountain. Thank God this car has four-wheel drive, I thought, as I clicked the little button on the gear stick which activated the additional two wheels. Now the problem was to find the Edwards' driveway on the right. According to the directions, it was a mile and a half up this road.

The driveway was indeed well marked; and I felt better about things as I stopped the car where the driveway ended, adjacent to a fenced-in field where, off in the distance, three horses were quietly grazing. I exited from my car, stretched briefly, and checked my watch. I was ten minutes early for my appointment with George Edwards at 11 a.m.

The place looked great, I thought as I leaned against a split-rail fence and looked around. There was a small, red, hexagonal structure about fifty yards up the hill with another hundred yards between it and the top of a knoll. As I turned to the right, I noticed a narrow road that branched off to the left and went downhill. There was a thin man, about 5'10" tall, who was walking up it. The man acknowledged my gaze with a brief wave of his right

4

hand, and then he lowered his head as he continued walking up the road. Must be Edwards, I said to myself, and I left the fence and began walking toward him.

"Hi, I'm George Edwards," the man said as he stopped in front of me and extended his hand. "My wife Susan and I live in a stone cottage just down the hill from here. That little red building you see up there is what you're looking for. We're asking $500 a month for it."

"Sounds reasonable. My name is Jeff Peterson, as I told you on the phone," I said as he accepted my handshake. "Can we go see the place?"

"Just follow me," George replied as he rounded my blue 1992 Subaru station wagon and headed up the hill. Half an hour later we were again back at my car where I opened the front door on the passenger side and reached into the glove compartment for my checkbook.

"I'll take it, Mr. Edwards," I said as I closed the door and looked up at him.

"Please call me George," he responded as he stepped back from the car and smiled shyly.

"Fine, George. This place is exactly what I'm looking for. Let me write you a check so I can start unpacking."

"Sounds good to me. Write it for June, and a $500 damage deposit. You can have what's left of May on me."

"Let's see," I said as I looked off in the distance and tallied the figures in my head. "I think that comes to $1,000. Who do I make the check out to?"

"Me, George Edwards. I'll be back after lunch with a lease and the phone numbers of the local utilities. I kept them all in working order. All you'll need to do is call each utility and have the account put in your name."

"Great," I said as I handed George the check. "I hope I'm here a long time and that we become good friends."

"I know Susan will want to have you for dinner soon. I'll ask her about that at lunch and let you know when I come back in the afternoon."

"I'll be here," I said as I reached out again to shake George's hand. George gripped it firmly and then turned to walk back down the drive. I watched him for a brief moment, and then moved to the back of my car where I unlocked the latch to the back door so as to begin the job of lugging my things up the hill.

George Edwards returned at 1:30 p.m. with the lease, the phone numbers, and a turkey and Swiss cheese sandwich and a Coke. This is just the place I need, isolated, in a quiet, beautiful setting at an affordable price, I thought to myself as I said goodbye to George for a second time and returned to my little house. By three o'clock that afternoon things were in pretty good shape. Brenda can make the place look homey when she comes for a visit, I concluded as I walked over to the corner of the small living room where I had left my guitar. One of the things I planned to do in these mountains was to rekindle my love affair with folk music and the acoustic guitar. So I took my first trip to the top of the knoll to serenade all the wildlife that cared to listen.

*   *   *

It took me a good while to acquire additional friends other than George and Susan Edwards. In many ways, that was understandable. To begin with, I wasn't feeling very social. In fact, I was rather self-absorbed, existing within a psychological cocoon which I had spun for my protection. I was also a single man, living by myself with no kids in school, and I was certainly not attending a church. That latter situation eventually changed, however, due to the strangest of circumstances.

It started at work. I began my stay in the North Carolina mountains by taking April and May off. During that time, as I indicated to you earlier, I explored the area on foot, in my car, and I played my guitar. Aside from the Edwards who were most kind in taking me under their wing, I remained pretty much to myself. The time alone, especially the walking part, was good for what hurt me. However, as the end of May approached, I decided it was time to look for work.

I interviewed for various jobs at Blue Ridge Propane, Mountain Satellite and Electronics, and Charleston Forge. I finally accepted the job at Charleston Forge because it offered more money—$6.50 an hour with good benefits. I was hired as a quality control inspector.

Charleston Forge is a metal furniture making company in Boone. They make beds, tables, chairs, baker's racks, coffee and end tables, and an assortment of other furniture. My job was to stand at the end of the assembly line and check for flaws in the finished product. Mostly this meant spotting parts that were not welded together properly or places on the metal that needed to be touched up with paint. It was the first time I had worked for an hourly wage since high school.

The work wasn't bad, and the people in the plant were quite pleasant, though again, I mainly kept to myself. I was pleased my life was taking on a routine. Work Monday through Friday from 8 a.m. till 4 p.m., which left the weekends free for hiking and further exploration of the area. It was a new life, a different life, a little lonely and boring at times; but I wasn't ready for much more than what this new life offered. My self-confidence had been shattered, and I was plagued with self-doubt. The simple rhythm of this new life got me through that first summer.

Things changed quite dramatically on the second Saturday in September. I left my home in Bethel early in the morning to hike on Roan Mountain, one of the few places along the Appalachian Trail where you are above the tree line for extended periods of time. When I returned late in the afternoon, I found the house had been thoroughly cleaned from one end to the other. It gave me an eerie, strange feeling, as well as a puzzling one. I called Susan Edwards to see if she knew anything about it, which she did not. She and George had been out most of the day visiting friends in Todd, a little community east of Boone. The next Saturday it happened again. This time I had gone to an Appalachian State football game. When I returned, I found supper all laid out for me—chicken potpie, peas, mashed potatoes, and a slice of apple pie. This is weird, I thought as I cleaned up the dishes after eating and set them aside at the end of the counter to be returned to my mysterious benefactor.

The third Saturday in this unusual sequence of events I was determined to get to the bottom of things. After breakfast, I read my novel, A.J. Cronin's *A Pocketful of Rye*, till about eleven o'clock. Then I took my guitar, two Coronas, and a sandwich to the top of the knoll.

They arrived a little after 2 p.m. I recognized their faces immediately as they walked toward the house. They were two ladies from work, although I didn't know their names. They were bringing up another dinner from their car, which was parked at the end of the driveway. I had taken the precaution of hiding my car behind the barn that was between the parking area to my place and the Edwards' cottage.

They were surprised to see me and a little flustered. "Hi, ladies," I called out with a smile as I approached them with my guitar. "I was wondering what was going on here. This is so nice of you. By the way, my name is Jeff Peterson."

"Well, we knew you was living by yourself and new to the area from talking to folks at work. When we discovered you lived just up the road apiece, we couldn't resist helpin' out a bit."

"And for that I thank you very much. The potpie was delicious last week. Now please help me with your names. I should know them, but I'm so bad about names. You are?" And I directed my attention to the short plump woman, the one who had just spoken to me, with the round face and the gray hair tied in a bun.

"Oh, yes, my name is Miranda Hodges," she said. "My husband is Ralph Hodges. He's an electrical contractor, but he's soon to retire."

"Nice to meet you, Miranda," I replied with a smile. "I bet your husband is looking forward to his retirement."

"He most certainly is, and this here is my friend Edith Townsend." Edith looked somewhat younger than her friend. She was a tall, hefty woman with long black hair that was becoming laced with gray. Her face was lined with wrinkles that could very easily have come from worry and care. It was the kind of face made beautiful by one who had devoted her life to others. She might have been in my high school year, I thought to myself, though she was probably a little older. I later learned that her husband was the janitor at the Bethel Elementary School.

"We're pleased to finally meet you, Jeff," Edith said as she lowered the covered dish and set it down on the steps.

"I apologize for being so standoffish at work."

"That's right understandable with you bein' new to town and that," Miranda said as she took a step toward the house.

"Well let's all go inside and get to know one another," I said as I reached for the door to hold it open for the ladies. They entered the living room and walked into the kitchen where they placed the dishes on the counter. The living room was small, but attractive in a rustic sort of way with pine wood floors that creaked as you walked over them, white pine paneling, a Vermont Casting wood stove, and appropriately arranged furniture—a log framed couch, a smaller sofa, rocking chair, and a wooden coffee table that was both scratched and stained with circular glass rings. Homemade bookshelves built up from the floor adorned the walls. The living room led into a small kitchen, and off to the right was a bedroom and the only bathroom. After returning from the kitchen, the two ladies sat at opposite ends of the couch. There had been no need for me to direct them into the kitchen with the food. They obviously knew it well.

"Are you this nice to all the strange men that come to work at Charleston Forge?" I asked as I leaned my guitar against the wall and sat on the rocker.

"Miranda and me go out pretty near every Saturday doin' missionary work for the church."

"That's really nice," I said. "Do you start by cleaning the house of the person you visit?"

"Not usually," Edith answered, with a shy grin, "but you bein' single and all we figured you could use it. Most times we just bring dinner."

"And what church do you do this for?"

"Oh, you've seen it," Miranda piped in. "It's the Sparkling Creek Missionary Baptist Church just down the road by Tester's."

"Pretty church. It looks like it's been freshly painted."

"It has," Miranda responded. "Just last year. We did it all on three Saturdays."

"Maybe you could play that geetar at one of our suppers," Edith interjected. "Folks sure would appreciate that."

"Now, that's an idea. I've never played my guitar at a church supper before."

"Are you a Christian man?" Miranda blurted out after a brief lull in the conversation.

"That's a complicated question, and I don't really know how to answer it," I replied softly with a warm smile. I hoped the smile and the gentle tone would help to ease any tension that such an ambiguous answer might produce, but I didn't succeed.

"You do go to church, now, don't you?" Miranda persisted.

"Well, I used to go every Sunday, but I recently stopped going."

"I think you'd like our little church," Edith said. "The membership is small, but the folks that go is so nice, and our pastor, Reverend Belcher, is a real fine family man."

"Didn't like the preacher?" Miranda cut in. She was obviously the feisty one of the two. I considered the question and laughed silently. I wondered whether I really did like my preacher right now. Thankfully Miranda didn't give me much time for further reflection. "Now, I wasn't trying to be nosey or nothin'."

"No, no," I responded. "I didn't take offense at your question. I was just thinking a little about my preacher. He was an alright kinda guy. I left because I had problems believing parts of the New Testament story."

"What parts?" Miranda asked with a somewhat challenging tone to her voice. "It's all true. God promises us it's all true. Name me just one part that ain't true?"

"Now, let me see. Do you know the virgin birth stories in Mathew and Luke?"

"Of course we do," Miranda snapped back.

"Miranda, please," Edith pleaded softly as she turned and looked at her friend. "Jeff may not want to talk about these things."

"Oh, don't worry about me. I enjoy discussing these questions, Edith. Miranda didn't mean any ill will. She's just interested in understanding why I no longer attend church."

"I guess so. I just hope we're not intruding," Edith said as she returned her gaze toward me. She made her point, however. Miranda's tone softened considerably.

"You do believe in the virgin birth, don't you now, Mr. Jeff?" Miranda asked. "I mean Mary had her baby in a real special way. The Lord, he come down, and it was all done by the Holy Spirit."

"I sometimes wish it would be that easy for all of us," Edith quietly commented to herself.

"Well, it's an interesting story. I just have a hard time imagining how the Holy Spirit was able to get Mary pregnant."

"That boy Joseph never touched our Mary. I can assure you of that," Miranda responded in a voice in which some of her original tension returned.

"Joseph was a male, and I'm sure he loved her very much."

"There's no way he hit a homerun with that girl if that's what you're athinkin."

"How do you know that?"

"Cuz they didn't play no baseball back then."

"You certainly have a point there," and I smiled warmly at her.

"We still would be most honored if you would come to our church," Edith interjected. "It's not far—just down the road as Miranda was asayin."

"I think I would like that," I said as I looked over at Edith and smiled. "What time is the service tomorrow?"

"Bible study classes starts at 9:45, and the regular service is at 11. As Edith said, we'd be real proud to have you join us." At that, Miranda stood up and Edith followed. "We brought you dinner again," Miranda continued. "I hope you enjoy it."

"I certainly will," I replied as I rose from the rocking chair, "and thank you so much for all you've done." I took the few steps into the kitchen and grabbed the dishes from the week before. "Here are the dishes from the last time," and I handed them to Edith. "See you both tomorrow at 11."

"You know so much about the Bible, Mr. Peterson," Edith said as she accepted the dishes with a shy smile that also radiated considerable warmth. "Maybe you could teach one of our Sunday school classes?"

"That's a very nice offer, Edith," I responded as I held the door open for the ladies to leave. "Ask me again when you get to know me a little better."

"Sure will, Mr. Peterson, and I want you to bring that geetar, you hear," she said with another warm smile. "I think you will make a wonderful addition to our church." I wondered about that last statement as I closed the door and walked to the kitchen to see what was on the menu for dinner. My mind was also racing and a little judgmental.

My two new lady friends represented different types of fundamentalists, I thought as I organized the dinner they had just left me. Miranda, the obvious leader of the two, was a fundamentalist by personality. Such people like to see the world in black and white. They demand clear, unambiguous answers to the complex problems of life, and their minds are good at segmenting their beliefs. The world of the Bible is separated out from other aspects of contemporary life. In fact, contemporary life is a problem. As God is squeezed out of modern culture, fundamentalists fear a loss of meaning. They sense they are losing their bearings, that liberal, secular culture is hurtling them into the dark abyss of nothingness, and they resent it. If one were to re-roll the cosmic dice and place Miranda in a different setting, she would be happy as an Orthodox Jew, an Islamic fundamentalist, or a member of a Hindu fundamentalist party in India.

Edith, on the other hand, was a person whose religion was motivated by love. She was attracted to the gospel teachings of Jesus, the sacrificial message of the cross, and the eloquent writings of Paul on love. She was a fundamentalist because she had grown up in such a church and knew nothing else. In short, like many people, she had inherited her religious beliefs. Taken out of the religious, social, and cultural setting of her youth, I could easily picture her as a sixties flower child or maybe even a Zen Buddhist.

Such speculation was fun and as I admitted above, a little unfair because I didn't know either one very well, but I had to laugh at the thought of Edith selling flowers on a street corner in San Francisco. I was looking forward to church tomorrow. It would be interesting to experience live a form of worship I had so often criticized without having a firsthand knowledge of it.

Chapter 2

The Mast General Store

BRENDA'S PLANE WAS LATE. I had been waiting at the US Air gate for forty-five minutes, and was beginning to become impatient. The arrival/departure board indicated another twenty-five minutes before the plane landed. The drive home to Bethel from the Charlotte airport was two and a half hours, and it was already 8:30 p.m. It would be a long night.

Even at this hour there were lots of people milling around the terminal. I finished thumbing through the copy of *USA Today*, which I found on one of the movie theatre-like seats in the waiting area, and decided to stroll the terminal corridors. It was by and large a happy, pre-Thanksgiving Day crowd—students with their backpacks, wives meeting their husbands, distinguished looking seniors arriving to visit their children and grandchildren. I was amazed at the number of foreigners. Charlotte was a far more interesting city than I had imagined from Boston.

The Charlotte airport was also easier to access than Logan, I thought as I passed by a gate check-in station on the left. The Sumner Tunnel that takes cars under the city was often a nightmare. There were just too many cars in Boston with drivers who were either in a hurry or otherwise uptight. This place was more laid back. The only things I missed in Boston were the Red Sox and the Pats.

Well, that's not quite true. I did miss my golfing buddies. Maybe I can join the Boone club in the spring or at least find a place to play regularly, I thought. You never had to worry about having something in common with a fellow golfer. The game itself was enough.

And then I was struck with an overwhelming sadness as I thought about Brenda and Thanksgiving. I missed my own parents. I had spent so many wonderful Thanksgivings at their homes in Athol and later in Sudbury. They had both died in 1992, within six months of each other. Dad went first from a long, debilitating bout of emphysema and congestive heart failure; and Mother, most probably, because she gave up on living after Dad died. They had been married for sixty-two years, an amazing achievement. Their relationship was both inspirational and touching.

I wondered if I would have left the church had they still been alive. Probably not. The only developmental problem I had as a young adult was fully separating myself from them. One thing I wanted to do in leaving Concord was to gain some distance from Rebecca, but I felt badly about that now. I wrote her a long letter of apology about four weeks ago, and she has yet to respond. She may never respond. I'm not really sure she wants a man in her life, certainly not me, and that's probably better for both of us.

I checked my watch again; ten more minutes before the plane was scheduled to land. I thought about buying Brenda a little welcoming present, but that was silly. It was out of character. I had always tried to express kindness in other ways. I did, however, start walking back to the gate.

The plane touched down at 8:57 p.m., and Brenda soon emerged into the bustling waiting area. She was wearing jeans, a green turtleneck, a gray U-Mass sweatshirt, and running shoes. When her large brown eyes finally located me, she broke into a wide grin and came bounding over to greet me. "Hi Daddy, you look great," she said as she threw her arms around me.

"It's so good to have you here, Sweetheart. How was the flight?" I inquired as I released her from my grip and looked down at her, smiling. She was an extremely attractive young woman, I had to admit. About 5', 4" tall, 130 pounds and constantly fighting to contain it. She had long brown hair, a round face with a dark complexion, one that always carried a nice tan, and a full figure.

"Fine, Dad, except that it was late. Sorry about that."

"No problem," I responded as I led her around the corner in the direction of the baggage claim area. "There certainly wasn't anything you could do about it. Do you have a lot of luggage?"

"No, just my usual blue duffel and this backpack," which she carried on her shoulders.

"That's good. I'd like to get off as soon as possible. We still have a two and a half hour drive to Bethel."

"I can't wait to see your little house. Your letter made it sound precious."

"I think you'll like it. The setting is even better."

"What are the plans for Thanksgiving Day?"

"The Edwards invited us for dinner around 4 p.m. They are the people I'm renting from."

"How nice. I look forward to meeting them."

"I think some of their children and grandchildren will be there too."

"The more the merrier. Sounds like we'll have a good crowd," Brenda said as she stepped onto the escalator that took us down a level to the baggage claim area. We waited a few minutes for the bags to arrive, and then I picked up her luggage and we walked to the car. It wasn't long before we were on I-77, headed north to Boone.

"Tell me about your new place, Dad?" Brenda asked as she leaned her seat back a little to get more comfortable. "The Appalachian Mountains have such an interesting history. I'm excited to see them."

"As a lifelong New Englander, I was humbled to learn these mountains are the highest on the East Coast. Even higher than Mount Washington."

"You're kidding. I bet they're beautiful."

"They are. Almost all the peaks are wooded, but the hardwoods are diverse and the land lush and green. Lots of pretty streams, rolling farmland, fascinating rock ledges, impressive rivers. It's much like Vermont really."

"Will I meet some real live mountain people? I hate to say the word hillbilly, but that pretty much describes what I'm thinking."

"Those days are gone, Sweetheart, at least in our area. Boone is a small city of about 30,000 people with a major university. The rural area where I live is populated with people who have second homes. Tourists, money, and the ski industry have found their way to Watauga County, which has changed things a lot."

"It's hard to believe they have skiing here," Brenda said as she leaned her head back further, nestling it between the car seat and the window, a place that always seems like it will provide great comfort, but one where it is difficult to actually find the right spot.

"You will believe it when you see how cold it gets. Especially at night. In talking to old timers, I get the idea the weather in winter is much like it is in Boston. The ski mountains are already making snow and should be open in early December."

"When I come for Christmas, I'll bring my skis," she said with a yawn.

"Are you coming this year?" I asked with a note of hopeful expectation. "I thought you said you were going to Concord to be with your mother and then to New York to be with Hank to welcome in the New Year?"

"That's the current plan, but if you hang around long enough I'll be here for Christmas," she said as she closed her eyes and listened to the soft jazz that was playing quietly on National Public Radio. Normally she would have searched for a livelier station, but she was tired and the music was serving its purpose by slowly putting her to sleep.

I looked over at her closed eyes, her pretty face, and smiled. She's the reason I got myself into this professional mess, I thought as I returned my gaze to the road ahead. And with that, my mind was back in Cambridge, Massachusetts, at the Episcopal Theological Seminary, in the early spring of 1973. It was my last semester, and I was working on a paper which analyzed some of the long Jesus speeches in the Gospel of John.

As I was reading through a commentary by C.H. Dodd, a fellow senior and good friend joined me at the library table. One of the best things about my three years at seminary was the great friends I made and the spiritual community in which I felt privileged to live.

"What are you doing here at this late hour, Jeff?" my friend Roland asked, as he pulled up a chair. "I would think Rebecca would be wondering where you are." Roland, of course, was single and didn't have to worry about such problems.

"I'm trying to finish the research for the paper that's due in Martin's class."

"What's it on?"

"I'm analyzing some of the images in John that are found in the long Jesus speeches. You know—light, bread, life, living water. Sure is different from the Synoptics.[1] You think you're dealing with a different Jesus in a different setting with a different take on religion. John is certainly not based on an eyewitness account. With all these problems, you wonder about the historicity of the whole thing."

"You never quit, do you, Jeff?" Roland responded as he leaned against a chair and looked over at me.

"I don't because these issues raise important questions. What am I going to tell the folks in Weston when I start there in the fall? That John's gospel is based on an eyewitness? That's what they want to believe."

"You have certainly made it into a problem," Roland replied as he turned to face me with a disappointed look on his face. "When are you going to start reading scripture with your heart rather than the rational mindset of a lawyer?"

---

1. The gospels of Mark, Matthew, and Luke.

"I know that's a problem."

"You question everything, Jeff. You really need to make some hard decisions about next fall."

"I know I do, but I'm in too deep. Married with a precious kid already. I need a job. I don't see any other choices."

"Through the heart boy, through the heart. I'll see you later. I'm meeting the group at O'Briens for a few beers," Roland announced as he got up from the chair and turned to go.

"Have fun," I responded, and then I reburied my head in the Dodd commentary.

Brenda was still sound asleep beside me in the car. In twenty-five years, one thing about her hadn't changed. She slept so soundly and easily. I guess one thing never changed about me either. I never learned to read scripture with my heart rather than my head. Maybe the answer is to read the Bible as a whole person with both heart and head. That sounds like such an easy solution, but as soon as my mind gets involved all I see are contradictions and problems. I think what we really need are new stories. That would be a great project to get involved in at some point in the future, I thought as my mind refocused on one of my favorite Brahms symphonies on NPR.

*   *   *

"That was a wonderful day," Brenda said as she stepped through the door into the little red, octagonal house. It was nine thirty in the evening, and it was misting outside with the real possibility of turning much colder. Rain often preceded cold weather in these mountains. I was hoping for a few snowflakes to impress my Yankee daughter. "Will you make a nice hot fire, Daddy? I would love to sip one more glass of wine before going to bed.

Brenda ran upstairs to her bedroom to change into a nightgown, ski sweater, and her slippers. Though small, her room encompassed the entire second floor, and she loved it. It was cozy, and the view out of the eight little windows was different in each case and magnificent. The first thing she had done on Thursday morning was to make it into her room as if she planned to stay there forever. I had brought some of her things with me, and so she was able to hang pictures and high school and college memorabilia on the walls. She planned to buy curtains on Friday. I tried to explain to her there were no other houses within seeing distance and that curtains were not necessary, but she wanted to fix up the room her way and that was the end of the discussion.

She came downstairs, poured herself a glass of red wine from the five-liter box on the kitchen counter, and snuggled up on the sofa with a blanket. I was blowing into the firebox of the wood stove to speed up the process of ignition. I soon grabbed a Corona from the refrigerator and joined her in the living room. "Well, what did you think of the Edwards'?" I asked as I pulled up the rocking chair alongside the sofa.

"Great people. You did well, Dad, in getting this place."

"Isn't that Susan Edwards something? She looks so average—a stereotype of the small town, middle class housewife. Not too tall, not too heavy, pretty enough in her own way though not glamorous, and very deferential to her husband. And yet her paintings are amazing. George told me she takes in well over $10,000 a year in commissions."

"I liked the mountain scenes in the fog."

"She's so humble about it," I said with considerable animation in my voice. I guess it was no secret I thoroughly enjoyed Susan Edwards.

"Quite shy really," Brenda reflected. "Her daughter Jennifer looks just like her. I liked her too. She was a high school math teacher for a few years before Mikey and Debs came along. What about George? Have you guys become good friends?"

"Sorta. Unfortunately, George and I don't have much in common, but he's a kind, generous person. He likes antiques, puttering, studying his investments, nothing athletic. He also has an answer for everything. I don't think he has ever doubted a thing in his life, which makes him a little insufferable at times. But I enjoy helping him with projects around here. They repay me by having me over for dinner. It works out well."

"Oh, I ate too much, Daddy. Promise me you'll never let me do that again," Brenda said as she looked over at me with a wide grin. And then her tone slowly changed. It became softer and somewhat melancholy. "Did you miss not having Mom and Scott here?"

"Scott for sure. I don't know about your mother."

"She's not sure about you either. As a matter of fact, she seems to be enjoying herself alone. I'm really quite proud of her. She was so dependent on you."

"Professionally, anyway."

"No, in more ways than that. I'm just surprised she's doing as well as she seems to be."

"That's good. I certainly have no animosity toward her. There are even times when I wish she'd come down here so we could talk about the last five years. We never did that."

"Cuz you bugged out before there was a chance."

"We just never talked about our marriage."

"You never talk about Scott, either, do you?"

"There's no one here for me to talk with."

"Weak, Dad. Really weak," Brenda said as she smiled lovingly across at me. "You need to talk about Scott, and you know it."

"Okay, let's talk about Scott," I said as I looked away from her and directed my attention on the fire.

"I know you miss him. Are you angry about what happened?"

"Not angry. It was just blind fate. We won the lottery, and the prize was tragic. It left a huge hole in my heart," I said, as my eyes began to mist. "I don't think it will ever be filled."

"I know what you mean. I cried the other day when Hank and I were having lunch together. I guess I was thinking of coming down here and, of course, Scott wouldn't be around to bug the heck out of me."

"Scott didn't always bug you."

"No, not in the last few years, but he sure did as a kid. He was your quintessential pest."

"How is old Hank? Have you made any wedding plans yet?"

"Not yet, but I'm sure you'll be the first to know about any plans that develop. Hank will want to talk to you about it. We definitely need to make some plans because we both graduate in May. We've lived together for almost three years. It would be sad after all that to go our separate ways. But you're changing the subject."

"I know, but what else is there to say?"

"I guess not much. The stupid jerk could never ride a bike anyway."

"And yet, he wasn't really reckless," I added as I looked up at Brenda with eyes that were fighting back tears.

"It was so out of character. The guy was president of the Fellowship of Christian Athletes in high school. I would have given him ten bucks as a kid to hear him say the word fuck."

"A minister's son."

"Am I a minister's daughter?" she asked, looking at me with a wide grin.

"Nope, I don't think so. In a way, you are nobody's daughter. You were so self-sufficient and secure in your life as a child. You're just Brenda. Was it hard growing up with a father who was a minister?"

"Not really. You seemed a little boring at times, always interested in big ideas and things like that. But I didn't think about it one way or another. I give you lots of credit for making it easy actually. I once told Hank that you never brought that stupid looking collar into the house. I hate wearing tight things around my neck."

"You get used to it."

"And heck, if I wanted to skip church, I just spent the night with a Presbyterian. The only one who gave me hell about it was Scott."

"What a strange combination of qualities he had," I said as I placed the empty Corona on the floor.

"So many good ones," Brenda said as tears flooded her brown eyes that were as large as saucers. "Hold me, Daddy," she said as she lifted her face toward me. I got up from my rocker, joined her on the sofa, and placed my left arm around her. She nestled her head against my shoulder. I held her close and felt the tears that were trickling down her face. I wished I could cry with her. It would probably help a lot. I must be defective or something, I thought as I gently stroked her long brown hair.

After a moment or two, Brenda raised her head and with her right hand brushed the hair from her face. "I think I'm going to take the rest of this wine to bed and read through my scrapbook. I can't believe you brought it down here."

"I brought it to read myself. It's so much fun to relive your life."

"You're so thoughtful, Daddy. I love you."

"I love you, too, Sweetheart. Have a good night's sleep."

"I will if the wind stays calm," she said as she raised herself from the sofa. She bent over and kissed me gently on the forehead, picked up the remainder of her wine, and made her way slowly up the stairs to her bedroom. My heart broke as I watched her climb the stairs. It was so great to have her here. She was my only real contact with the past and so precious. Hank is a lucky man to have her, but he's a good guy too, I thought as I went back to my bedroom to fetch my novel. It would be another hour before I was ready for sleep.

*   *   *

My sleep was short but restful, no nightmares or fitful tossing, and when I awoke at my usual time of 6:30 a.m. I felt remarkably refreshed. Not having a nightmare left me with a sigh of relief because I had a persistent one, about this naked man, standing in a one-man receiving line, screaming at the passersby to take notice of him. And those passing by, men, women, and children all dressed in black, refused to look at him as he stretched out his hand to greet them. The people kept filing by; and he, in his screaming nakedness, was unable to reach them.

The dream needed little interpretation. It was a constant reminder of my past and my failure as a minister. But it was receding now, coming less often, and that seemed like a good sign. After a quick shower and shave, I dressed and went outside to gather wood for the stove. Although I was initially disappointed to find no snow on the ground, my spirits lifted with the thought that this would be a clear day.

The crackling fire and the smell of coffee and bacon on the stove aroused Brenda forty minutes later. "Smells great, Dad. I'll be down in a minute."

"No rush, Sweetheart," I called back. "You might want to wait till the place warms up a bit."

"That's okay," Brenda responded. "I'm getting dressed now anyway. Go easy on that breakfast, though. I'm still full from last night."

"Just bacon, scrambled eggs, raisin toast and coffee."

"Sounds like a lot to me."

"You can eat what you want."

"You know me, Dad. I'll pack it all away. Raisin toast is my weakness. Got some good jam?"

"Strawberry."

"Great! I'll be down in a jiffy." After a brief pause in our conversation while I attended to breakfast, Brenda called again from upstairs. "Hey Dad. Do you know what day it is?"

"Friday, I think."

"Yes, but that's not what's important. It's the day after Thanksgiving and do you know what that means?"

"I'm afraid to ask?"

"It means we shop."

"Along with all those millions of people," I responded in a tone that reflected my bemusement with Brenda. She has always been our best shopper.

"In Boston maybe, but not here. You couldn't have brought me to a better place to shop at this time of year. Are there any stores?"

"A few. Actually, there is one place I wanted to show you in Valle Crucis called the Mast General Store."

"Sounds great. We can start there."

"Start?"

"Get ready for a full day of it. Tomorrow is your day."

"Is that a promise?" I asked as I took the bacon out of the pan and placed it on a plate with paper towels to absorb the grease.

"Sure is, provided I find what I'm looking for."

"Do you know what you're looking for?"

"Nope. That's why we're going to shop." I smiled to myself as I reached for the bowl with the scrambled eggs and poured them in the pan. The entire thing sounded like a black hole to me, but at least Brenda was here. Her company was worth the shopping spree.

*　　*　　*

Valle Crucis is a tiny village in the northwestern corner of North Carolina. It is located in the Appalachian Mountain chain within Watauga County, about a twenty-five minute drive from Boone. It is a community rather than a town because the county does not provide it with legal status, but the three or four hundred full-time residents certainly think of it as a definite place. It is a simple community where folks are content to live simple lives, a place where many residents leave their homes unlocked when they are not there. In that sense, it has a 1950's feel about it, and yet it is not main street anywhere because there is no main street.

Like an old mountain man, Valle Crucis has character, a character that derives from traditional mountain ways and the influx of many interesting people from all parts of the country over the last thirty years. This melding of disparate cultures has produced an easy, open style of living that any newcomer recognizes immediately and comes to cherish.

The heart of this picturesque hamlet is nestled at the conjunction of three waterways—the Watauga River, Dutch Creek, and Clark's Creek. There is a small Methodist Church located there and a larger Episcopal Church up the hill toward Banner Elk that looks out over the central valley. A little elementary school sits in the center of the village, which is surrounded by an assortment of shops. The Mast General Store is located two hundred yards from the school. It has been the center of Valle Crucis community life for the past one hundred years.

This 10,000 square foot structure is painted white with green trim. Part of its charm is that it always looks like it needs a fresh coat of paint. A newcomer to the area will also be struck by the Esso sign that stands proudly at the far corner of the building near the main entrance to the store. That sign signals something important about the place. Time seems to stand still at the Mast Store, to tread water, while everything around it is churning and seemingly rushing headlong toward some unknown future. This sense of timelessness is another aspect of the store's great charm.

The first thing you encounter as you enter through double wooden doors, doors that fit together so poorly you wonder how they lock the place at night, is the post office to the left. "Do people actually get their mail here?" Brenda asked as she marveled at the hundred or more mailboxes made of metal and brass.

"The locals do. Do you see that old potbellied stove to the right with a bench and some old chairs around it? Many locals get their mail and then sit down on the chairs to read it. There's a group of retired men that come every morning to get their mail and trade stories."

"Do they also play checkers?" Brenda asked as she passed by the mailboxes and approached the stove. There was a checkerboard sitting on an old wooden end table which was placed between two chairs. "I love the bottle caps. I guess if they find there aren't enough caps to play with, they just go buy a Coke."

"Do you play checkers?" I asked with a grin.

"No, Dad. I shop. Hey, look at those gourmet coffees over there. A fancy smelling coffee would get me up fifteen minutes earlier tomorrow morning," Brenda said as she moved away from the potbellied stove, deeper into the store. "Do you ever shop here, Daddy?" she inquired in a saucy tone with a big smile on her face.

"Occasionally I come if I need a hardware item. You find that stuff in the back."

"Boring," Brenda responded with a smile. "Where are the clothes?"

"What are you looking for?" I asked as we strolled past an enclosed glass cabinet filled with pocketknives, fishing gear, small tools of various shapes and sizes, and an assortment of other practical items.

"Well, what I really want to get Hank while I'm in the south is a Confederate flag. I can see it hanging in his office next fall. First job, Jewish lawyer, member of the ACLU. It would be perfect."

"Interesting, although I don't think you'll find one here. I kinda remember seeing a few antique Civil War shops in my travels, but I couldn't tell you where. Perhaps we'll run into one if we drive to Boone."

"That will be the next stop. We'll look for one after we finish in here."

We spent the next two hours trying on parkas, looking at sweaters, and scanning various hiking guides and travel books. Brenda was tempted to purchase a coffee table book about Valle Crucis, but I convinced her, with a rather sheepish grin on my face, to put it on her Christmas list. The last place we visited was the shoe department where I bought her a new pair of hiking boots.

"This will guarantee that tomorrow is my day," I said as I handed the clerk my credit card and looked back at Brenda with a smile.

*　　*　　*

We left the store around noon, and headed toward Boone for lunch and more shopping. As we were passing the Mast Farm Inn on the right, one of the fine bed and breakfasts in the area, I turned to Brenda and said: "Maybe we better go back to the Store for a minute. You could buy Mom a Valle Crucis trinket for Christmas. She would love a Mast Store sweatshirt, don't you think? Something that symbolizes my new home."

"Stop teasing, Dad," Brenda said as she looked over at me with a grin that lit up her round, brown face. Her complexion would allow her to pass for a Native American. "I've already taken care of Mom's present."

"What did you get her?"

"I wrote her a short story."

"You're kidding. What a lovely idea. She will really be touched. What's the story about?"

"A little girl who lives in a fish bowl."

"I guess you know something about that."

"A little," she said while bracing herself as the car made its way around a ninety-degree switchback.

"What's the story about?"

"Well, this little girl lives in a fish bowl with her mother, and she gets tired of everyone looking in at her. So she swims down to the bottom of the bowl, surges upwards, and tries to leap out. She makes it on the fourth try, only to find herself in worse trouble as she flops on a wooden dresser top and gasps for air. She looks back at her mother who is unable to help her and starts to cry.

"The next day the ten-year old girl who has been feeding her finds her on the dresser, concludes she is dead, takes her outside, and throws her on the ground. The tiny fish languishes there on the ground for what seems like months until one day a young prince discovers her."

"Is Hank the young prince?" I asked as I looked over at her and smiled.

"He thinks he is," Brenda shot back with a chuckle. "Hank got into my computer and changed the prince all around. I had him as rather homely looking with a sweet smile, but Hank made him into a handsome, swarthy stud."

"I love it," I said as I eased the car to a stop where the Broadstone Road intersects route 105 across from the Ham Shoppe, a quaint family restaurant that specializes in luncheon fare.

"Anyway, the prince picks up the little fish and takes her back to his castle where he nurtures her back to health. Strangely, I guess because the prince has a magic touch, the fins on the little fish become limbs and before you know it a beautiful princess is formed. I didn't let Hank mess with this part of the story. A prince inherits his position, which means you never know what you're going to get, but a princess must earn hers. They are always beautiful. Anyway, I guess you can figure out the rest."

"Of course the prince marries the princess, they have many children, and live happily ever after," I said as I accelerated to pick up speed after turning left onto 105.

"Of course."

"Oh how I love happy endings," I said with a smile.

"I'm not sure about that. After they have their second child, the princess wants to reconnect with her mother so she takes the prince's horse and rides back to her old village. She eventually finds her previous home and her mother, considerably older and swimming alone, slowly in the bowl. The princess reintroduces herself and relates her story to her mother. As she finishes, her mother sadly confesses:

'Oh, my precious little minnow. I have missed you so. For many years I have been trying to gather the courage to leap from this fish bowl, but now I'm afraid it's too late. My life will soon be over, and I will never know what I could have become.' Or something like that."

"Wow," I said as I looked over at Brenda with a big lump in my throat. "Your story ends with a bang."

"I hope Mom won't be offended," Brenda said as she returned my gaze.

"She'll be touched you care that much."

"I hope so. The good thing is that she is starting to venture forth from her fish bowl."

"Maybe your story will encourage her to take larger steps."

"That's my hope."

"Will you send me a copy?"

"I will if you find me that Confederate flag."

"We'll look for it after lunch."

*　　*　　*

The shopping trip was great exercise, lots and lots of walking, and a learning experience for me. What was amazing was that we actually purchased very little. I bought hiking boots for Brenda as you saw and that was the extent of my damage. She bought lots of little things for various friends, but nothing major. It was interesting for me to find out what some of those old friends were doing. We did eventually find a Confederate flag for Hank in a trinket and souvenir type shop in Boone. I guess that meant the trip was successful. Brenda could get everything else on her list in some New York mall.

We didn't get back till 6:30 or 7 p.m. which was amazing in itself. I couldn't think of a place in Watauga County we missed. I was planning to take her out for dinner, but she was tired and not very hungry, so we had leftover turkey the Edwards' had given us from the previous night, frozen spinach, and lots of red wine. I was really getting to like red wine. I started drinking it a few years back for my heart. My GP in Concord suggested it during a routine physical following my fiftieth birthday, bless him, but I had to be careful. It was not like drinking beer, and I am not a heavy hitter.

I discovered during the five days Brenda was with me that she liked it too. We were sitting around the fire again, sipping wine, and talking about her soon to be launched teaching career, when all of a sudden, out of the blue, she changed the topic and brought up something she had obviously intended to talk about while she was here. It seems that she didn't want to leave Bethel without some understanding of why I left the church. "Do you really hate the church that much, Daddy?"

"No, Sweetheart, I don't. What brought that up all of a sudden?"

"Well, you left in such a rush and everything."

"I know I did, and I wish I could do it differently now. The problem is that you can never take back past actions. But I don't hate the church. In fact, I still feel the Christian Church is one of the great pearls of Western Civilization. It stands for what is best in humans, for what is most precious and good about human life.

"You'll be interested in this. I was reading recently about the special attraction the church had for women in the early years of its growth and development. The church appealed to women because it raised their status, and because of its doctrines outlawing abortion and infanticide. Infanticide was common in the pagan world which usually meant the killing of female babies. Crude abortions, and that was the only way they were performed back then, led to the death of many women."

"Times change. I guess what's right and good for one time in history may not necessarily apply to a later period," Brenda responded as she looked over at me intensely.

"That's certainly true, but what is constant and good is the church's support for individual people, for developing human potential, for making the world a safer and more civilized place to live. That's the church at its very best."

"If all this is so great, then why did you leave? That's what I'm trying to understand," she said as tears began to form in her eyes.

"Is that really an important question for you?" I responded rather defensively, and maybe even with some meanness. "The church never played a very important part in your life."

"Yes it has, damn it. Please don't put words in my mouth that aren't true. Your leaving the church disrupted my life, it changed everything." She was sounding like a little girl, my little girl, the little girl who was mad because I had missed an important activity she was participating in, and it broke my heart.

"I'm sorry about disrupting your life," I responded gently and with real sorrow. "I'm sorry for hurting your mother and the other people in the congregation that counted on me. As I just said and have thought so many times over the last year, I wish I could do it all over again."

"Why did you ever become a minister in the first place?"

"That's a good question. It's a shame you never met my next-door neighbor Trudi. She was a year older than me, but we were best friends.

One day after school Trudi came over to the house, and told me she wanted to marry Fred. I was probably eight or nine. Anyway, guess what my role was?"

"You were the minister, of course."

"How did you guess?" I said laughing. "The point is I had wanted to be a minister from as far back as I can remember. Your Mom was thrilled about the prospect of becoming a minister's wife. I had no real problems with belief until I went to seminary. I was fascinated with my studies, but also questioning. Before I knew it the three years were over, and you were a part of our lives. The simple truth is I needed a job."

"So it's all my fault."

"Come on, Sweetheart. That's not fair. You are one of the best things that has ever happened to me. I was so excited when you were born. But to get back to your question. I have learned over the last six months that my belief problem was not what drove me from the church. I had no problems talking about a God of love, a God that forgives and shows mercy, or a Jesus who was a passionate proponent of peace and economic justice. What I have learned is that the real problem was psychological."

"What do you mean by that? You seem so normal and wonderful to me."

"It all started with the Vietnam war."

"You've never said a word about that war."

"Very few people wanted to talk about it, both then and now."

"I'm fascinated with that period of our history and know so little about it. It's just a big blur. People say the sixties was a really cool time, but I have no idea why. And Vietnam was so controversial. Tell me about your experience. I bet it was exciting."

"Terrifying is more like it."

"Do you feel like talking about it?"

"It's a long story."

"They're often the best, and we're certainly not going anywhere soon."

"You may not believe it, but I've never told this story to anyone before."

"You're long overdue, Dad," Brenda said as she looked over at me with a reassuring grin.

"I guess you're right. Well, as you know, I graduated from Williams on June 6th. My draft notice came eight days later. Everyone seemed to be getting drafted in the summer of 1967."

"Did you ever think about Canada? Wasn't that where people went when they opposed the war?"

"Yes it is, and I did consider it. I thought about getting a PhD in philosophy there, and then staying if that's what it came to. But I wanted to get married, and I was worried about Gigi and Gramps. He was a top executive with the Ford Motor Company in Detroit, and very conservative. I didn't want him trying to stop the marriage, which would have happened if I was in Canada."

"What would Mom have done?"

"Probably come with me, but it wouldn't have been fair to put her in that situation. I also felt that if I didn't go someone else would have to go in my place which wasn't fair either."

"The old minister in you," she said as she shifted her position to get more comfortable.

"I guess so. Anyway, when you got drafted back then, it was either the Army or the Marines. I chose the Army, and went for a blue-collar experience. I could have gone to Officer's Training School, but I wanted to make friends with people from different backgrounds.

"Once I was drafted, everything happened so quickly. I started my training at Fort Benning, Georgia on June 30th. By the end of July I was a private in the U.S. Army, with a shaved head, and a piece of paper that said MOS-11B. Almost everyone in our group received the same assignment. It meant I was to become an infantryman, and I was scared shitless, if you pardon my French.

"I later learned that it was a little unusual for a college graduate to be assigned to the infantry because the Army desperately needed clerk typists at the time. So the bureaucracy screwed up. The tales of bureaucratic ineptitude in the military were legion, but the Army certainly knew how to fight a conventional war."

"Did you go to Vietnam immediately?"

"Almost, but first we were shipped to Fort McClellan in Alabama for advanced training."

"Was it interesting being in the south all that time?"

"It certainly was hot, unbearably so really. And yet I have to admit that it was interesting for a kid who had never been south of DC before. We had some free time in Alabama, so I often went out with some of the guys. I was amazed to find Alabama so green and lush. Quite pretty really."

"Was it hard adjusting? You hear all kinds of horror stories about boot camp."

"It wasn't that bad. The discipline and physical training were a lot like football practice. It was a little difficult to make friends at first, though. I was just so different from the other guys in the company. It's the only time in my life that my football career was a big asset. When word got around that I was an All Conference wide receiver from Williams College, things turned around. The guys in my company had no idea where Williams College was or that a good high school team from Texas could have given us a run for our money. It was a nice myth which helped me gain respect.

"I finished up at Fort McClellan sometime in the middle of September and received a fifteen day leave before going to Vietnam. I returned home to Sudbury, and your Mom took a week off from Smith. It was a special week, and we became engaged on that last Friday."

"The pressures of war. So romantic! That kind of thing seems to happen a lot."

"I guess so, but one thing happened that week that wasn't typical of most wars, although it certainly says a lot about the sixties you are so interested in. While we were there, I took your mother to a protest rally on Boston Common. It was our first pot experience."

"Wow, Dad. Did Mom smoke with you?"

"Actually neither of us did, but while we were sitting on the Common singing protest songs, the stuff was being passed around all over the place. When we left the rally that afternoon to catch the subway back to Riverside, we had an interesting confrontation. Right before the station at Park Street, we ran into a group of middle-aged men who were shouting obscenities at us students for protesting the war. They called us cowards, traitors, deserters, and they flavored their comments with a string of four- letter words. Three or four came right up to us, shouting in our faces, and waving the American flag."

"Did you take a swing at one?"

"No, no, of course not, Sweetheart. I grabbed Mommy's hand and scrambled into the station as quickly as possible. Afterward, on the subway, your mom was furious at them. I just smiled at the wonderful irony of the whole thing. Here I was about to go fight for them. They should have been slapping me on the back."

"What about the wedding? Were you able to make any plans before you left?"

"Not really. There wasn't enough time. I drove your mom back to Smith on Sunday, and I flew out of Logan for San Francisco on Monday morning."

"I bet it was a teary goodbye."

"It was, especially because I was really beginning to get scared. I had a hard time leaving Northampton because it meant I was going to war the next day. Anyway, to get back to your question, I told Mom to make the plans and that we would do it as soon as I got back. Combat tours were for twelve months. I arrived in Vietnam on October 4, 1967, and was home in early October, 1968."

"That doesn't sound so bad."

"A lot can happen in twelve months. I landed, after brief stops in Hawaii and Guam, at Tan Son Nhut Air Base in South Vietnam around 4 p.m. on October 4th. We were quickly bused to Long Binh for processing where I was assigned to Charlie Company, Fourth Battalion, Ninth Infantry Division which was headquartered in Tay Ninh Province.

"It was at Long Binh where I met my first Vietnamese. I was eating dinner at the enlisted men's mess, and this older woman came to clear the table. I say older because there was no telling her age. Her face and hands were badly wrinkled, she was emaciated and slightly stooped, and her smile was missing two front teeth. Reality closed in on me. As I looked up from my plate and returned her smile, I was jolted into the awareness that this was more than a war zone. It was a different planet from the playing fields of Williams College and the gentle, loving words of your mother so recently ringing in my ears.

"Tay Ninh Province bordered Cambodia and the southern-most entrance to the Ho Chi Minh trail. The guys in our platoon claimed that the terrain was similar to the American southwest, although never having been to the southwest, I couldn't swear to it. It was for the most part flat, dry, and lifeless, at least during the dry season. It was also isolated. There were no homes, factories or villages anywhere near our camp.

"It was our job to stop the infiltration of North Vietnamese regulars into South Vietnam which meant that for the most part we fought a conventional war, pitched battles against uniformed NVA soldiers. We did extremely well in this war. We had the know-how, the firepower, helicopters, and the troops to get the job done. There is no equal to the United States military in this type of conflict.

"You said earlier that the Vietnam War was controversial. Unfortunately, there was another war, the war in the countryside, in the villages and hamlets of South Vietnam. From what I heard, we had no idea how to win that war. It was next to impossible to tell who the enemy was, and we didn't have a well-defined strategy to deal with the problem. We should have made it clear to the South Vietnamese that this was their war, but we didn't. It was this second war that we lost."

"Interesting, Dad, but too academic. I can read all about that in a book. What happened when you were actually fighting?"

"I'll never forget my first battle. I guess no soldier ever does. They helicoptered us right up to the Cambodian border where we established a fire support base on top of a hill that overlooked a major NVA infiltration route. There we dug a series of trenches and underground bunkers. The idea was to make us as invisible as possible so that we would be in a position to ambush the enemy. Well, it didn't take the NVA long to figure out our position, and they came after us one night a few days before Halloween.

"The attack started with a barrage of mortar and rocket fire. Shells were exploding all around us. And then they opened up with their AK47 rifles. AK bullets have this high-pitched whine; it's a horrifying sound. The air was filled with explosive sounds and bursting light that looked like the climax to a Fourth of July celebration. The ground was shaking around us.

"I really thought that this would be my first and last fight. They seemed to be on top and all over us, but then outside support arrived. The officers ordered us into the bunkers we had dug the day before, and then they blasted the NVA with VT artillery. Vertical Time artillery sends out shells that explode before they hit the ground. So here we were safe in our bunkers while the advancing NVA were dropping like flies. It worked. We lost twenty or thirty guys. It was a bad night, but NVA casualties were enormous. It was always difficult to estimate their loses because they carried as many bodies away as possible. But the next morning we found fifty or more dead NVA soldiers around our perimeter.

"VT tactics or whatever you call them sound like the stuff that goes on in a video game."

"It was no game, Sweetheart. That's what it was like, night after night for eight months. They mostly came after us at night. I came to dread the setting sun. You would lie awake wondering if this was the night you'd get hit. The really scary part of combat was waiting for something to happen.

Once a battle was in progress, there was too much to do to worry. You acted on instinct and training."

"You said eight months. I thought you were there for a year."

"I was, but my stay in Tay Ninh was broken up with a week's R&R in Bangkok, Thailand. There were three places you could go for R&R—Hawaii, Australia, or Bangkok. All the guys would pass around magazines while we were sitting around at camp so we could check out the girls from each of the three places. I chose Bangkok because of my interest in Buddhism."

"Sure, Dad. What were you looking for? A little naked yoga!"

"That would have been nice, but I really did want to see a Buddhist temple."

"Did you?"

"Several."

"What else did you do there?"

"Are you sure you want to know?"

"No, I'm not, but unfortunately you piqued my interest."

"It's your dirty little mind running on overdrive," I said as I looked over at her and smiled. "Maybe it would be best to get the truth out quickly. Yes, I did meet a girl there. Her name was Lec or at least that's what I called her. She had a long Thai name that I couldn't pronounce and I can't now remember."

"I thought you were engaged to Mommy?" she asked with a sly twinkle in her eye.

"I was, but I had also been living with men for the last eight months under some pretty stressful conditions. I wanted a warm body and to feel emotion again. I was also excited about losing my virginity. I used to lie awake at night wondering if I would die a virgin."

"You mean Mom was that much of a prude."

"Let's just say she had a set of internal rules that she adhered to faithfully, and that premarital sex violated those rules."

"I have always respected Mom for living a principled life."

"Me too, but back then a few of her rules were a little disappointing. But, let me finish the story. The Army flew us to Bangkok in a commercial jet and then bused us from the airport to a tourist center in the city. While on the bus, this NCO briefed us on Thai women. I will never forget it. I was flabbergasted at his directness. He advised us to stay away from streetwalkers, that the girls in the bars were licensed and had passed medical examinations. How about that!"

32

"You underestimated our military bureaucracy. It was efficient in both love and war."

"They were at that. While we were at the tourist center, they had each of us draw a number from a hat to choose a hotel. There were ten official R&R hotels in the city to choose from. I picked the Rich Hotel which turned out to be fine, though a little boring. It operated like an American establishment, just like the name suggested.

"I hailed a cab from the tourist center to take me to the hotel, and I got this nice driver in his late fifties. I wish I could remember his name. He spoke some English, was very pleasant, I didn't meet a Thai person who wasn't friendly; and so I took another suggestion from the NCO and hired him for the week. It was incredibly cheap.

"After a shower and shave, I asked the driver for a tour of the city. Eventually we ended up on Patpong Street where all the bars are. We went from bar to bar, and it was fun to watch my fellow GIs in action. Because I was picky, it took me most of that first day and many Thai beers to find Lec. She was employed at a bar called the Roxy, which, again as the name implies, was too American for my tastes. I was looking for a more Oriental experience."

"Was she pretty?"

"Beautiful—thin, with dark features, long brown hair, and this invitingly round face. Quite stunning really. She was about my age, maybe a year or two older. She took me everywhere. The only thing we didn't do was see the *King and I*. It was banned throughout the country."

"What was Bangkok like?"

"Kinda like Venice, with an Asian flavor. It is built around a system of canals which we explored on a barge. We went to the royal palace. It was obvious Lec had great respect for the King and Queen. It was the first touristy place she took me. She claimed they were rarely in town because most of their time was spent in rural areas championing economic development projects. We also saw several Buddhist temples and some practicing monks. I left with the distinct impression that Buddhism was strongly adhered to by most of the Thai people. You could see its effects in the friendly manner and gentle nature of the people."

"What about the food? Was it good?"

"Exotic, or at least the stuff that I remember eating. Most of the restaurants we frequented were sidewalk cafes. At one place this young dancer came to entertain us. She was dressed in a long, flowing blue wraparound, with a red, ornately decorated top. She danced around our table with incense candles as a means of paying tribute to some minor Hindu deity."

"Did you ever write or see that girl again?" Brenda asked in a somewhat accusatory tone. She was far more interested in Lec than the Hindu dancer.

"Nope, but I thank her to this day for the wonderful week. She immersed me in Thai culture and introduced me to the best sex I have ever had."

"La, la, la, la, la, la," Brenda chanted with a grin as she covered both ears with her hands. Then her expression changed and a disapproving look crept over her face. "That's not very fair to Mom."

"I know, Sweetheart. It's really quite cruel, but it's true. After Scott was born and she was the mother of two healthy children, she shut down emotionally as far as sex was concerned. She responded loyally to my advances as if it was part of her job description, without much passion or seeming interest, but let's leave Thailand so that I can finish the story." It felt a little strange, awkward really, to be telling Brenda the story of my affair with Lec, but awfully good to get that dig in about her mother. I think subconsciously I wanted to tell Brenda this part of the story for that very reason.

"Please do. I think the less I know about your Asian fling the better."

"What comes after Thailand is the hardest part. It happened so quickly after I got back. The guys in my combat unit were tight. We were so different, and yet we faced death together every day which created a depth of loyalty among us which is hard to explain if you haven't experienced it.

"I had several good friends in the platoon and one best friend named John Murley. We called him Murls. In so many ways Murls and I were like Mutt and Jeff. He was a puny kid, about 5'8," and no more than a hundred and sixty pounds. He came from rural Georgia where his father was a peanut farmer. The Army got him at nineteen, a little less than a year after he graduated from high school. He arrived in Tay Ninh a month before I did.

"He was a sensitive guy and really funny. We often slept outside on air mattresses, watched the shooting stars overhead, and talked till the wee hours of the morning. He told me about what it was like when the court forced the desegregation of his elementary school. He admired the first black student there, Shirley something I think was her name, and they became good friends in high school. He also told me all about peanut farming, which is what he wanted to do when his tour in Vietnam was completed. We talked a lot about careers back then. I, especially, was searching.

34

He kept encouraging me to become a minister. Maybe I did so to honor old Murls. We looked after each other and promised to see that our bodies were shipped home if the worst happened.

"Anyway, about two weeks after returning from Thailand, we were ordered on an intelligence gathering operation. Our mission was to move out from the base camp in concentric circles looking for evidence of the enemy—trenches being dug, throwaway packages of AK shells, that sort of thing. The idea was to set an ambush for them, but instead we walked right into their trap.

"It was about 10:30 on a hot Tuesday morning; and we were walking about, scattered over a small area, looking for clues. All of a sudden the entire world exploded around us. The NVA had us in a semicircle ambush. Bullets were raining everywhere. I was next to the radioman, who called for choppers. He ordered me to pop a smoke grenade to pinpoint our location.

"In the meantime, I heard three of our guys screaming. They were badly wounded. Then Murls joined their chorus. He was fifty feet ahead of me and lying on the ground. I ran to him. He had taken two rounds in the stomach and one in the neck. I cradled his head while bullets were whizzing around us, and he bled all over me. Oh, Sweetheart, this is so tough," I said as tears welled up in my eyes. Brenda leaned her head against my shoulder and gave my left hand a reassuring squeeze.

"His lips struggled to form words, but no sound came out. Only a gurgling noise, and then his eyes lost their focus. I panicked and screamed out in anguish. 'Live, asshole, live. Don't you dare die on me, you motherfucker.' And I held him tighter, hoping to squeeze life back into him, but his eyes were closed and there was nothing. Only his wristwatch continued to tick, that stupid watch some girl had given him as he was leaving the country. I woke up for years in the middle of the night hearing that damn wristwatch ticking, always ticking.

"A minute or two later I heard choppers, maybe it was less time than that, it was hard to tell amidst all the confusion and my grief, but I suddenly felt some relief that I could fulfill the promise we had made some months ago. I picked him up and started walking as fast as I could toward the opening where the choppers had landed. I hadn't gone more than fifty yards when our Lieutenant Lecka ordered me to drop Murls and help another buddy, Private Allen, his first name was Lark—we called him Meadowlark, to the choppers. Lark had been wounded badly in his right leg.

"I did as ordered, delivered Meadowlark to a medic and then started back after Murls. Lecka saw what I was doing and ordered me on the chopper. When I kept walking, I was in a daze really, Lecka leaped in front of me and rammed a M16 in my stomach. "You're coming back with me, Peterson. Let the dead bury the dead.""

I stared off into the fire, fighting back tears, and Brenda reached for my hand again. I sensed that she was crying too. "I like that Lieutenant Lecka," she finally said. "He saved your life."

"Murls is still in Nam, Sweetheart," I stammered through my tears. "That's what mattered to me then."

"What matters to me now is that we're here together, that you're my Daddy, and I love you."

"Thank you, Sweetheart," I said as I struggled to gain control of myself. "You're really right about Lecka. He wasn't a bad guy. In fact, he had been a friend, but I never spoke to him after that unless it was a necessity. I went dead emotionally. For the last three months I was there, we did similar sweeps, set up ambushes, interdicted the NVA, but it's all a blur. I charged the enemy without thinking or hesitation and fought with a take no prisoners attitude. Vietnam taught me to be a damn good killer, and that thought disgusts me, even now. The really sad thing was that I remained emotionally dead long after coming home in October 1968."

"That's the part I just can't get over, that you didn't talk to someone about this horrible stuff. Did you have a psychological death wish or something?" Brenda asked as she took her head from my shoulder and looked at me with eyes that were pleading for understanding.

"Nobody wanted to talk about Vietnam when I got back in '68, honey. Mommy sensed from time-to-time that I had had problems over there, but she never asked me to talk about it. That's what I meant when I told you our communication problems started from the outset. We developed a pattern of not sharing what was closest to our hearts and that pattern was so destructive to our marriage. We got along great as professionals, but not when it required sharing what really mattered. I don't blame Mommy, Sweetheart. It was mostly my fault. My maleness."

"It's just so hard to believe that a professional caregiver would be so inept at taking care of himself."

"Actually, I did okay until Scott died. Then the whole thing came down on my head. All the guilt and anger from Vietnam returned and merged with Scott. Your mother and I held each other for that first week and then

I faced it all on my own. She walked and talked with her friends. They forced her to deal with her guilt and grief. The guilt part is so irrational, but it must be dealt with before you can heal. I kept my own counsel and focused on my work. I covered over the searing scars of Vietnam by getting married and going to seminary. When everything collapsed two years ago with Scott's death, I catapulted myself out of the church and fled to these wonderful mountains."

"What are you doing now to resolve all that hurt?"

"I have been reliving Vietnam and Scott's life every day since I arrived here. Going over all the relevant stuff over and over again."

"Is it working?"

"Yes, Sweetheart. Slowly. I'm slowly learning to release the guilt and anger."

"I love you, Daddy, and I'm so very proud of you."

"Can you forgive me for what I did?"

"I did that long ago."

"Thank you, Sweetheart. That means more to me than you will ever know." And I finally shed long overdue tears. This remarkable young woman, with her simple directness and obvious concern for my well-being, had pierced my heart. She had been doing it all day with the result that compassion and emotion were surging through me for the first time in months. For the next few moments, she allowed me to sit there in silence, in that semi-darkened room where the lights from the fire danced along the walls and furniture. I hoped the darkness hid my tears, but I wasn't sure. After five minutes or so of this silence, she quietly got up from the sofa, kissed me gently on the cheek, and made her way upstairs to bed. I sat there for another half an hour drinking up all the warmth and love of the past day like a parched nomad who has finally located an oasis.

*   *   *

I awoke well rested and refreshed for a second time. It was just so good to have Brenda here. Maybe it was all that exercise from the shopping yesterday, I thought as I stepped outside into the open air. Little stars were still dimly shining in the predawn sky before the morning sun would delete them from ordinary awareness. I was excited because the stars signaled the weather would be nice for Brenda's last full day in the mountains. As I have learned over the years from experience, it often rains here in November. We had been lucky these last few days.

I was also excited because today was my day, and I planned to take advantage of it. I was taking her on a hike to a place I called Delphi. It was about a thirty-minute walk from the house. I had stumbled upon it last July on one of my long, solitary walks that had become such an important part of my therapeutic routine.

We had a light breakfast, packed a lunch, and were ready to leave the house by about 10 a.m. Brenda had on her new hiking boots and an expectant look on her face, a look of hiker's determination, as we circled around the back of the house, passed the Edwards' on the left, and headed for open land with Grandfather Mountain several miles off in the distance. Our trail was one of those rare places in the Appalachian Mountain chain where you hiked with open views above the trees. It was up one hill and down another along pastureland that wasn't actively farmed, although you occasionally saw a small herd of grazing cattle.

"You said we were going to Delphi at breakfast. Where did this place get the name Delphi?" Brenda asked about ten minutes into the hike.

"I named it. The place reminds me so much of Delphi in Greece. It's a little spooky, very mysterious, awe inspiring, so different, and private. Your Mom and I were there almost thirty years ago, the summer before I graduated from seminary. Nana and Gapa gave us the trip. It was our real honeymoon. Actually, you were there too—in the oven."

"Was Mom pretty when she was pregnant?"

"I thought she was. She never did look all that pregnant—either with you or with Scott."

"It's that thin, girlish figure. I guess I came from your side, except you're as thin as a rail too. Are there any chunky ones in the family?"

"Nana."

"Yes, Nana was full figured, bless her heart. She had the most beautiful face and the plumpest little body."

"You could do worse."

"I know I could, Daddy," she said as she smiled over at me. We were quiet for several minutes as we walked along an old animal trail where the grass was limp and brown, the result of several hard frosts over the last few weeks. At a fork in the trail we turned right, heading south, where the old trail went through a group of hardwood trees that was too large to call a clump and too small for a forest. Emerging from the trees after an easy ten-minute walk, all that remained was to ascend a steep ridge and peer down.

"This is so awesome," Brenda said as she stopped at the top of the ridge to catch her breath and look down into the bowels of Delphi. As she scanned the scene below, she reached for the water bottle she was carrying around her waist. "Want some, Dad?" she asked.

"No thanks, Sweetheart. I'll have something after we get set up."

"Explain to me again why you named this place Delphi?"

"Because it's beautiful in an eerie way. Completely surrounded by mountains as you can see."

"It looks like a large volcano crater from here."

"Precisely. When you get to the bottom and look up and then all around, it reminds me of that wonderful temple in Greece. You'll have to go there some day." As Brenda turned ninety degrees to take in the scene from another direction, I reflected further on why I found this spot so special. It's a place where the silence closes in on you, where there is magic in the air with hawks soaring high above looking for prey, and tiny goldfinches and wrens flitting along the ground looking for material to build a nest or food to nourish their families. It's the kind of place a person can do some good thinking and emotional healing. That's what I use it for. I consider it my private Appalachian temple.

After some reflection on her own, Brenda turned toward me and broke the silence. "Well, let's get down there so I can explore it. Oh, I see your little tent off to the right."

"It came in real handy this summer. Remind me before we leave to take it back with us. I won't be needing it till next spring." As I began my descent down the ridge, I picked up sticks as I went. It was always good to have extra wood for the fire. Brenda followed my lead.

"I can smell your old fire," Brenda said as she dropped the sticks she was carrying inside a blackened area that was surrounded by rocks. There was a gentle breeze blowing and the ground was still a little damp from the rain on Thursday which probably accounted for the charcoal smell. "It's so quiet here. We're all alone in the world, or that's how it seems," Brenda commented as she smiled over at me.

"Sounds like the lyrics to a John Denver song. I bet he found lots of places like this in his travels," I said as I unloaded the wood I was carrying and placed it beside the fire pit.

"You remind me of Denver sometimes, Dad," she said as she laid her pack on the grassy floor and prepared to sit next to the fire. "What songs would you write? You've got plenty of time and talent."

"Sounds like a fun idea. Maybe I'll write a song someday. I'd write about the same themes—love, the environment, harmony in the universe. We see the world pretty much the same way, though I might throw in an anti-war song or two. The Bob Dylan thing."

"You and Denver are just a couple of cockeyed optimists," Brenda said with a laugh as she settled in alongside the fire pit. I took some dry newspaper from her pack, arranged the smaller sticks on top of it, and lighted the fire with a wooden match. Then I joined Brenda beside the fire, and we both fed it in silence, adding larger sticks as the tentative flames gathered strength. Eventually I broke the silence.

"Do you know what I'm thinking about, Sweetheart?" I said as I looked across at her with a wide grin.

"A penny for your thoughts."

"I'm thinking about your remarkable athletic career in high school."

"I got lucky now and then."

"My proudest moment as a parent came at a basketball game you played in ninth grade. Do you have any idea what I'm getting at?"

"That asshole coach we had?"

"He was at the center of it. I can't remember who you were playing."

"I think it was Acton if I know where you are going with this."

"Probably was. That short, little bowling ball of a man had been screaming at the refs for the entire game. Some girl on your team was called for traveling; and he exploded, running off the bench to confront the referee. I guess you had had enough because you ran after him, grabbing him by the arm, and shoving him back down on the bench. What did you say to the guy? I wish I could remember his name."

"Coach Harper. We called him the screamer. I told him if he left the bench again I would walk off the floor and quit the team."

"It helped you were the high scorer."

"Maybe."

"Did he ever speak to you about it?"

"Nope, but he did start behaving himself."

"I know. That was what was so special about the whole thing. I just can't believe you did it."

"I like to surprise you Dad," she said as she got up from the ground and gave me a big wink. "I'll be right back. I have to go pee." Upon returning, she brought two beers and a bag of chips.

I reached across to clink beers with her and broke into another wide grin. "Do you remember the only time I spanked you? I ended up splitting my fraternity paddle."

"You must have really spanked me good."

"Not really. It was an old paddle."

"You only spanked me once?"

"I don't think I ever spanked Scott. In fact, I know I didn't."

"He was a goody two-shoes."

"You could be naughty. I can't remember how old you were. Probably about five. We had a stick shift Toyota wagon, and you discovered if you put the key in the ignition and turned it, the car would lurch forward.

"The first time you did it was on a Saturday morning. I was cutting the grass, and out of the corner of my eye I saw the car lurch forward. At first I thought it was an optical illusion, but then I saw you laughing hysterically behind the wheel."

"I told the examiner when I took my driver's test at sixteen I had been practicing for a long time."

"When the car moved forward again, I ran and got you out."

"Was that when you went for the paddle?"

"No, but I gave you a good talking to. I decided not to tell your mother."

"That was a good idea. She would have driven the car to the dealer and traded it in for an automatic shift."

"Things got worse on Sunday. When your Mom and I came back from a late afternoon reception at the church, the babysitter was in a panic. The car was six inches from the house."

"And I got the paddle for that? I didn't even hit the house."

"No again. We put you in your room with a stern scolding. Three days later I came home, and the car was in the woods. You got it started, and then learned about neutral. It rolled down that little hill.

"Your Mom had put you in your room; and when I came in with the paddle, you took off. I chased you out of the house and finally caught up with you in the yard. Boom went the paddle, it split in two, you screamed out, and then started laughing hysterically. You couldn't believe you had split the paddle. I couldn't either, and started laughing with you."

"I'm just a hard ass, Dad."

"I guess so, but it worked. You never did it again."

"You and Mom were great parents. I took a psych class last semester on dealing with kids. They say the teenage years are tough, but you guys had no problems with it. Do you know why?"

"I have no idea."

"Because you were deeply involved in our lives, but you kept your mouths shut. You came to all our games, and we did fun stuff as a family on vacations. And there were no sermons. You never lectured us. I guess you got that out of your system on Sunday."

"We did ignore a lot of little things, but remember that lecture about pot?"

"That's the point. You never told me not to smoke it, but you scared the hell out of me about driving and smoking. Remember our sex education class? That was the best."

"Not really."

"Well I was about thirteen, in bed, listening to the radio. You came into the room, sat down on the bed, and stared at me. You just stared at me. You didn't say a thing. Finally, I said something like: 'Hey Daddy-O. What's up?'"

"Not much Sweetheart. Did you have fun at the dance?"

"It was great."

"What did you do?"

"Well duh! I danced with a few guys and talked with my friends."

"Well, you know, Sweetheart. You are now at an age when you can get pregnant."

"From dancing, Dad? Maybe I need to teach you a little about sex."

"I was that bad."

"Pretty inept. I hope you did better with the sandwiches. I'm starved. It's time for lunch."

We left Delphi in the afternoon with a renewed closeness between us. Reliving her childhood had been a good way of doing that. Not long after we arrived at my small mountain home, Brenda presented me with an early Christmas present, a book of 365 chicken recipes. The best part was she helped me use the book to fix a gourmet meal. By the time we left for the Charlotte airport early Sunday morning, she had made my house into a home with simple decorations she hung on the walls and placed on tables around the house. More importantly, she made me feel love again.

She helped me learn a lesson that I had tried to help others understand who were grieving that you do not honor the dead by dying with them.

Chapter 3

Sparkling Creek
Missionary Baptist Church

IN SEMINARY SCHOOL AT Harvard, I received considerable training in clinical psychology. I continued my study as a minister, and saw many parishioners with a wide variety of problems over the course of twenty-five years in the ministry. The trouble was, when hurting myself, I was totally unable to understand my situation.

What became obvious later was that I went through a full-blown midlife crisis. As people travel through life, personality change is a natural part of the process. For many, transitions through life occur naturally with a minimum of pain or disruption. For me, my inability to deal with John Murley's death, the death of Scott, the failure of my marriage, and the collapse of my career came together to intensify the transition to midlife and to make it into a crisis.

I probably should have sought out professional help, but as I suggest above my judgment was clouded. Time, a disciplined regimen of long walks, and my guitar helped me to gain some perspective. Brenda, as you just saw, reactivated my heart. She helped me to feel human again. My healing continued when I met my first friend. I made an appointment to see Greg Williamson in early February, not quite a year following my arrival in the mountains.

Father Greg, as he likes to be called, is the rector of the Holy Cross Episcopal Church in Valle Crucis. I wanted to meet and introduce myself to Father Greg because I thought I could be of some help to him. I told him at that first meeting a little about my previous history with the church and that, although I wasn't interested in becoming a member of Holy Cross, I was available as a friend who had "been there before" if Greg ever needed one.

"I like your proposal," Father Greg said in a deep voice that displayed a slight trace of a Southern accent. Father Greg is a short barrel of a man with dark hair and a well-manicured beard. He is a happy, warm workaholic, the type of priest who is destined for greater things if that is his ambition. His relative youth, late thirties, maybe early forties, was strongly in his favor, I thought as I prepared to leave the church office.

"An objective friend," Father Greg mumbled as he stood up from behind his desk. "I will certainly give you a call."

"I hope so," I replied as I extended my hand toward him. "I wish I had had one." It was 5:30 p.m. and already quite dark when I left his office for the trip back to Bethel. These winter months could be lonely ones, I reflected as I turned left from the church parking lot. I was happy, however, to be expanding my circle of friends even if the process was taking place ever so slowly, one friend at a time.

I didn't hear from Father Greg for nearly four months and then a call came with an exciting prospect. The Valle Crucis Community Park was hiring an executive director. The Board was also looking to extend the mission of the nonprofit corporation to include a nature conservancy. Father Greg was hoping to recommend me for the job.

And I was excited about this new opportunity. Things were going fine at Charleston Forge, and the company had in fact given me a nice raise after being there for six months. I had sought out such a job when I first arrived in Boone because I wasn't feeling very sociable and because I thought it would be interesting to get to know working people. The same instinct had driven my enlistment decision a quarter of a century earlier. But now I realized I needed something more. This new job involved maintaining the Park (landscape work), and running a small nonprofit corporation—fundraising, coordinating volunteers, and setting up the nature conservancy.

The job appealed to both my idealism and my love of making things beautiful. I had always wished there had been more time for gardening in my previous life. The only negative about this new job was the salary. I would be making about the same as I had at Charleston Forge, although the Park was closed during the winter which meant that a major portion of my responsibilities would cease for four months during the year.

I was on edge during the interview only because I wanted the job so badly and because the Board grilled me with difficult questions. At one point I was forced to admit that I knew little about establishing a nature conservancy. A few members seemed to react negatively to the fact that I had left the ministry.

I left the Board meeting at 7:30 p.m. in a rather dejected mood, thinking that there was no way they would hire me. When I arrived at home, I noticed the answering machine light on my telephone was blinking, a rather rare occurrence in my household. In the time that I had left the meeting at the Valle Crucis Elementary School and arrived home, it couldn't have been more than half an hour, the President of the Board had called. I returned the call immediately and received the unexpected news that I was hired. The great thing in my favor was the low salary. I was the only candidate for the position. My start date was July 1st.

My first meeting after the interview with the Board President, a single woman, in her late forties, who is a nurse in the emergency room of the Watauga Medical Center, had gone extremely well. I left feeling optimistic that we would work well together and relieved that she didn't want me to worry about the nature conservancy until after the Park closed for the winter at the end of October. That left fundraising and landscaping as my major responsibilities. I particularly enjoyed the latter because it was outdoors and because the hours were flexible. This allowed me to play my guitar in the morning and work at the Park after lunch until dark if need be. The Park was especially beautiful at dusk with the sun setting behind a western peak, creating a fragile light which made for an atmosphere of stillness and peace. It was my favorite time to walk the five-eighths of a mile track that encircled the Park perimeter.

Working in the afternoon and early evening also brought me in contact with members of the Valle Crucis community. This has been an unanticipated benefit of the job. It enabled me to meet several people who live in Valle Crucis. It was how I really got to know Sandra and Greg Williamson, for example. It interested me that they too were making new starts in the mountains. They had come from the eastern part of the state and were only married four years ago. It was a second marriage for both; and because the new marriage had not produced children, they were free to have picnic dinners at the Park. They did it once or twice a week during the summer months, and Sandra soon got in the habit of bringing extra food for me. With no place to go after work but home, I was delighted to join them.

About a week after the annual Fourth of July celebration, a big day at the Park with civic ceremonies, a community picnic, and fireworks for 500 spectators, I decided to leave a little earlier than usual. It was 6:15 p.m., and I rushed off to check my mail at my new box at the Mast General Store. The Store closed at six thirty. I got there in plenty of time, it was less than a five-minute drive from the Park, looked in the window of my box and saw that I did indeed have mail. After sorting through the junk and a bill from the telephone company, my eyes stopped short as I spotted a thin envelope addressed in Rebecca's handwriting. I decided to open that one at home with beer in hand.

The letter was short, and matter of fact. She wanted a divorce. As I sat in the rocking chair in the living room of my tiny house, a rush of sadness flooded through me. It wasn't that I still loved her. In fact, I couldn't even remember when I last felt that way. As I explained before, our marriage had been a professional partnership more than a loving relationship which itself was sad.

I was sad because the longest chapter in my life had ended in failure. All that remained was to draw up the divorce papers. I wrote her a letter that night in the same tone as the one I had received—no further apologies, and no expression of what I was feeling that night as I reflected on our failed marriage. I merely expressed my wish that we handle the divorce without lawyers and that we split our shared assets down the middle. In the main, this involved my pension with the Diocese of Massachusetts and a housing fund that we had set up when I started my first job in September 1971.

The housing fund was created at the suggestion of the presiding minister of that first church. He explained to us what we both already knew but had yet to face, that housing came with the job of ministry but that we would both be out in the cold upon retirement or if I ever left the church. Not long after receiving my first paycheck, I started contributing seventy-five dollars a month, twenty-five dollars each to three mutual funds. By the time I left the church in April 1995 the total sum of my monthly contribution had increased to $600. For her part, Rebecca contributed from her salary when our expenses allowed. When our parents died and we inherited some money, we established two more mutual funds and added to the three original investments. On December 31, 1995, the only day of the year in which I paid much attention to our investments, the combined worth of the five funds was slightly in excess of $950,000.

As I finished typing the letter on my computer, I hoped the terms would be agreeable and that the money Rebecca received would help her get started with a new life. Whatever animosity I had previously harbored against her was now gone. I wished her the best, that she succeed in her new life, whatever that new life turned out to be; but I couldn't help feeling sad as I sealed the envelope that things might have worked out differently.

*   *   *

Spiritually, there is a large part of me that is Taoist. Taoism is the philosophy developed in China in the sixth century B.C. by Lao-tse. It is a philosophy derived from Lao-tse's close observation of nature. As I drove to the Sparkling Creek Missionary Baptist Church, I thought about my failed marriage in Taoist terms. Life is a continuous process of dynamic growth, the ancient philosopher taught. The very essence of life is change, nothing ever stands still, which was comforting. I felt ready now to embrace the changes that had come into my life. Lao-tse also taught that dynamic change results from the blending of paradoxical opposites—the coming together of yin and yang to form something new and exciting. Out of these opposites emerge new and beautiful patterns or so the philosophy goes. I wondered whether such a synthesis would emerge tonight at church. I had promised Miranda and Edith that I would attend the revival there at 7 p.m.

It was the second week in August, and revivals were scheduled for the entire week. Wednesday was bring a guest night, and though not really a first-time guest, I had been to the church several times over the last twelve months, I thought that this was the most appropriate night. It was also the one my two lady friends had requested that I attend. They had come by the house for a brief visit the previous Saturday.

The Sparkling Creek Missionary Baptist Church is a small church that sits fifty yards off of George's Gap Road. It is painted white with a pale blue trim, and there are several attractive stained glass windows on both sides of the church building. Inside everything is made from wood; wooden benches as pews, oak wood floors, pine paneled walls, and a small wooden altar, simply adorned, with a pulpit on the right side as you face the altar and a lectern for scripture reading on the left side. An antique piano is located at the front of the church on the right just below the pulpit, and there is a small balcony in the back for the choir.

I arrived at the church at 6:55 p.m. and hurried inside so as not to be late. I spotted the two couples immediately. They were seated in the middle of the church on the pulpit side. I squeezed in next to George, Edith's husband, fondly greeted both couples, and scanned the simply printed bulletin. From the look of things, it seemed that this would be nothing more than a traditional church service, and I was disappointed. I was expecting more from my first revival.

A hush came over the church members as the Reverend Belcher and a visiting minister entered from a side door, came to the middle of the church, and turned to face the congregation. The Reverend Belcher gave the invocation and introduced the first hymn. I had always been impressed with the volume of singing. Maybe it was the small size of the building, but in fact it was more than that. This congregation of seventy-five or so members could certainly belt out a hymn. The volume from my 500 parishioners in Concord paled by contrast.

After the first hymn, there was a scripture reading, a long drawn out prayer, an anthem by the choir, and the sermon. It took the sermon for me to realize that this service would be special after all. It was delivered by the visiting minister, the Reverend T. Sammy Paxton, who specialized in revivals. He toured a three-state area, visiting a different church each week.

T. Sammy looked as if I had cast him for the part. He was a sinister looking man, thin as a snake, with a hawk-like nose. A fierce energy emanated from his face, causing me to wonder whether a smile would be able to erase his censorious demeanor. As he stood before the congregation, fire and brimstone raged from a raspy little voice that was at times so quiet I had to strain to hear, and then by the flip of a switch that voice began to rise until T. Sammy was actually shouting at his audience, toxic fumes spewed forth, as he demanded that each member of the congregation admit their guilt and call on Jesus for forgiveness. Edith, along with several others in the congregation, was silently sobbing. As I surveyed the scene, the ones not crying seemed to be mesmerized. I saw no one who was asleep, bored or otherwise distracted. Attentions were riveted. You couldn't avoid the glaring eyes. It was like traveling down a narrow highway and facing a car with its bright lights on. T. Sammy certainly held your attention. It was an impressive performance.

Following the sermon the main show began as members of the congregation came up to the front of the church one at a time to make a testimonial. The first four or five confessed to some small transgression and then proclaimed that Jesus had come into their lives to change their sinful ways and to make them into new people. I sat there intrigued, my analytical mind spinning in a judgmental fashion. T. Sammy had set the tone.

After these initial performances, a hush fell over the members for a second time. It was as if the entire congregation had been waiting for this moment. A man in his mid-twenties came forward. He was obviously nervous, and when he started speaking it was impossible to make out his words. At this point a young woman stepped forward to join him, looking more than a little pregnant and obviously the man's wife. The woman smiled up at her husband, took his hand, which calmed him down considerably, and gave him the confidence to begin his story again.

The congregation did not seem surprised by the story. He confessed to having an affair over the last six months which had abruptly ended when Jesus came into his life. The healing love of Jesus had saved the couple's marriage and changed the man into a new person. I sat there listening, admiring the man's courage, my judgmental mind softening as the drama unfolded.

What happened next was unbelievable. The whole congregation came up right then, the man had barely finished his story, to forgive the man and congratulate the couple. The service had no formal ending, that was it. There was a spontaneous outpouring of love and forgiveness for that young man which pervaded that tiny mountain Baptist church. You could feel its presence. It touched even the cynic from Massachusetts who had come to honor his two friends and to see a good show.

The ladies shoved me forward to meet the young couple. "Lookey there," Miranda said as she poked me in the ribs. "There's his mother-in-law ahuggin' on him." I was introduced to Kelley and Hal McLean, the young couple that had set off this spontaneous outpouring of compassion and forgiveness, Mrs. Eggers, the mother-in-law, the Reverend T. Sammy Paxton as well as a host of friends of Miranda and Edith, some of whom I had seen before at previous services. I left the church at 9:15 p.m., after attending a reception of dessert and coffee in the church basement, feeling elated and strangely optimistic about life. I had even enjoyed my conversation at the reception with T. Sammy, discovering that he could in fact smile and that there was a pleasant person behind the harsh demeanor.

On the way home and afterwards in my rocker sipping a glass of red wine on the porch overlooking the tall, uncut pasture grass that was my front lawn, I reflected on the experience. There was no question that something real had happened that night at the Sparkling Creek Missionary Baptist Church. Love is real. It is a part of the created universe. When a person's everyday concerns and focus of attention are dramatically redirected away from self and toward another, love is encountered and experienced within. As Martin Buber's famous book *I and Thou* teaches, it originates outside the individual but it flows inward, and it has a very special quality that distinguishes it from normal human activities and experiences. Unlike other human energies that diminish when shared, love expands and grows the more deeply it is experienced. It is so different from anything else that emanates from an otherwise self-centered individual that many associate this energy with the divine. God is love is a frequent conclusion that is made.

All this ran through my mind, a type of reflecting I relished, a practice that used to be a frequent exercise in my work and spiritual life but that had become less common now. I enjoyed immensely the sipping of the wine, the slow rocking, and the gentle breeze that helped to relieve the lingering heat as it caressed my face and upper body. The moon was three-quarters full, and it popped in and out of white, billowy clouds that slowly drifted by. It was an appropriate setting to conjure up such divine thoughts, I concluded.

And yet I also knew that Jesus could not save that marriage, any marriage for that matter. The skeptic in me wondered how long the divine fix would last, how long would that young man remain faithful to his beaming, pregnant wife? One hoped forever, but statistics and common sense suggested the possibility for a different outcome. The point is that we save our marriages daily by the decisions we make. I knew the truth of that statement from my own, very difficult experience.

I also knew that genuine religious experience reinforced bad theology for many Christians, not only fundamentalist Baptists. I remembered an older man in my congregation who frequently wept after receiving communion. The forgiveness and love symbolized in that service overwhelmed this man. It made real and totally believable the creeds and the main outlines of the New Testament story.

The Nicene Creed floated through my consciousness. I wondered how the love experienced at the communion rail as my parishioner reached out to Jesus proved that God was male, a father; that Jesus was this God's only son; that the mother of this Jesus was a virgin, that this man Jesus actually died and came back to life; and finally that this creature, fully human and fully divine, whatever that means, ended his time on earth by ascending to heaven. The Ascension had always tickled me. I wondered if many Christians had ever paid attention to the first chapter of Acts where it is described. There the story is told that as the disciples and others looked on, the physical body of Jesus rose into the air as if he was traveling in a hot air balloon. Where did this body go, where is the heaven in which it ended up, and why wasn't this spectacular event attested to in history books? The only account is in the Book of Acts. Obviously, the love encountered by my parishioner at the communion rail or the love that spread throughout the Sparkling Creek Missionary Church proved none of these points of doctrine.

Enough of this theology, I thought, as I filled my wine glass one more time in preparation for a different communion. The softness of the night, the starry sky, and the gentle breeze brought to mind all the good things that have been happening in my life over the last twelve months. Fulfilling work, new friends, and some understanding of my recent past were blessings that proved a new beginning was possible. The only thing missing was a woman to keep me warm at night. I was finally ready to think seriously about dating.

Chapter 4

The Auction

It took another fourteen months for that to happen. I was working at our annual auction, which was held each year on the first Saturday in October. The idea was to catch as many tourists as possible who were here to see the leaves and looking for something to do. It was the most important fundraiser of the year, and it had kept me working overtime for the three weeks prior to the event, contacting merchants for donations and collecting items given by our small community of donors.

I arrived at the Valle Crucis Elementary School at 7 a.m., along with several volunteers, to unload the items for auction from the Mast General Store truck, and to set up the school cafeteria. This involved moving tables from the center of the room to the outer walls and arranging chairs for customer viewing into the middle of the room. A separate group of volunteers also came early to organize a food booth at the rear of the cafeteria for the purpose of feeding two hundred or more people breakfast and lunch.

The formal bidding was set to begin at 9:30 a.m. As I was carrying an antique lamp into the building, one of the last pieces of furniture on the truck, a middle-aged woman stopped me with a question. "Excuse me, please. Do you work here?"

"Yes, what can I do for you?" I said as I rested the lamp on a cafeteria table.

"I think I would like to buy this box of books. Do you know when it might be auctioned?" the woman asked, smiling up at me.

"Usually we get to that type of thing after lunch. Can you wait that long?"

"Oh, sure. I'm never in a hurry to leave an auction. Thank you very much."

"You're most welcome," I replied as I picked up the lamp. "Boxes like that usually go for well under five dollars. So hang around and your patience will be rewarded."

"What a bargain! There's a whole course in Russian literature here."

"Great. I'll talk to you later," I said as I rushed off to deposit the lamp near the stage. It was 9:28 and time to begin. We had just made it, and I marveled at our volunteers. Everyone had a role to perform. The same people had been putting on this auction for so many years that very little overall direction was required. It just seemed to come together at the appointed time. As I walked toward the small stage at the front of the room with lamp in hand, I ran into Fred Rose, a local plumbing contractor and member of the Park Board. Fred was over by the stage rearranging several items of furniture into a more coherent order.

"Not a bad turnout for this time in the morning, Jeff. I'd guess there's more than a hundred."

"Looks about right," I responded as my eyes quickly glanced around the room. "There should be plenty more as the day progresses."

"I hope so," Fred said. "We can use the money!"

"We sure can, and I don't want to be hauling all this stuff back to the Mast Store warehouse when the thing is over. Thanks for all your help," I said as I handed Fred the lamp and turned to step onto the stage.

"No problem," Fred replied as he started to move toward the back where the collected furniture was stored to find a place for the lamp. "I'll be here most of the morning. Just holler if I can be of further help." I smiled at Fred one last time as I stepped onto the stage to engage the microphone system. The two auctioneers, who were talking along the center aisle with members of the audience, saw me take the mic, ended their conversations, and moved toward the stage.

"Good morning, and welcome to our annual auction. My name is Jeff Peterson, and I am the executive director of the Valle Crucis Community Park. Let me begin by thanking Carmen Pagnoli, the principal of the Valle Crucis Elementary School, for allowing us to have the auction in this cafeteria. Previously, I understand, the auction was held at the Park, but for the last several years we have been inside at the school as a precaution against bad weather. You never know about mountain weather," I said with an impish grin.

"Is Carmen here?" I continued as I surveyed the crowd. "Yes, there you are toward the back. Please stand, Carmen, so that we can give you a hand." While a polite applause ensued, I went on speaking. "Carmen not only gives us his cafeteria, he helps clean it afterwards." The applause grew louder, and many faces in the audience smiled.

"Next, I want to introduce Mrs. Karen Swift, another important person to our organization." Karen smiled shyly and nodded to a smattering of clapping hands and a few whoops. "Karen runs the food booth. She has coffee, donuts, and bagels for those of you who missed breakfast or who happen to get hungry bidding today. They also have a very inviting lunch menu. Karen is just one of many volunteers who make this auction possible." The applause deepened.

"So that we can get the show on the road," I concluded, "let me bring to the stage our two auctioneers. They are also volunteers; and, as you will soon see, they are very good at what they do. On my left is Dr. Sandra Farley. Many of you know Sandra from her work with Blue Ridge Community Theatre. She has had important roles in several productions, the most recent being the first wife in the *King and I*. Sandra also teaches in the psychology department at ASU. If you do a good job bidding up her prices, you might get her to sing for you. That in itself is worth the price of admission. Dr. Farley," I said as I smiled at her and stepped from the little stage to give her a hug. As I moved the few steps toward her, she immediately grabbed the mic.

While laughing, she said: "I'm sure you all noticed there was no charge for your admission this morning. As a result, with regard to my singing, I'm afraid you will get what you paid for." She handed the mic back to me and gave me the hug I had intended for her.

I returned to the stage, and turned toward Ralph Mueller. "Speaking of priceless, Mr. Ralph Mueller." Ralph smiled, bowing deeply to acknowledge the polite applause and a few snickers from my silly attempt at a joke. "In addition to auctioneering, Ralph calls out square dances at the Apple Barn and is the owner of Blue Ridge Glass and Mirror.

"Before turning the mic over to them, I want to thank you all for coming this morning. The money you spend today is the lifeblood of our organization. For those of you who don't know us, the Valle Crucis Community Park is a twelve-acre park that sits adjacent to the Mast Store Annex and the Candy Barrel, and we also operate a small nature conservancy for our area."

I stepped off the stage, handed the mic to Sandra, and made a quick exit for the food booth. I needed a cup of coffee. The wonderful aroma of it, emanating from the area around the booth, caused me to quicken my pace. I poured myself a cup and leaned against the back wall to watch the proceedings begin. It was the first break I had had since arriving at the school that morning. My first cup of coffee too. Morning coffee was important in turning me into a human being.

The crowd seemed to be enjoying Sandra. She is a natural ham. I looked around and saw lots of familiar faces. These good people had come, checkbooks in hand, to support our work. I was touched as I stood there watching the proceedings unfold. There were lots of visitors too. The mood in the cafeteria was chatty and enthusiastic. I felt optimistic it would be a good day.

As my gaze reached the right side of the room, I locked onto the woman with an interest in Russian literature. Where was she from, I wondered? She certainly wasn't local. She looked younger without the reading glasses, and I silently laughed at my fixation with age. Pretty silly really. She was quite professional looking, I concluded as I continued to admire her, with a face that was animated as she focused her attention on Sandra. The professional look must come from that short black hair. I tried to remember her eyes. It seemed they were soft blue, a remarkable combination really if my memory was correct, but it was impossible to tell from this distance. The angle was wrong too. I could only see the side of her face. Very pretty really. I was thinking of walking over to get a closer look, when abruptly my pleasant reverie ended.

"Jeff," Sally Robinson whispered from the registration table not far from where I was standing. "Can you come here a minute?" And I was off to lend assistance or answer some minor administrative question.

*   *   *

The next time I checked my watch it was 1:15 p.m. Serving lunch had been hectic, but things had gone pretty well. The Park volunteers were old pros at this sort of thing. What got my attention was the lady with the books. She had just purchased them for the staggering sum of $3. I watched her smile shyly as she acknowledged her victory, and my feet began inexorably moving in her direction as Ralph Mueller called out bids for a donated television set.

"Quite a bargain," I said as I pulled up a metal chair constructed for a third grader and sat down beside her.

"Not bad, not bad. I did all right for myself, don't you think?" she replied as she returned my smile. Her eyes really were soft blue, just as I had imagined a few hours back. They reminded me of two robin's eggs peering out from a rounded nest. It was a dumb thought, I knew, but lots of dumb thoughts were surging through me right then. She was both understated and stunning. Much prettier than my initial impression in the morning. "Your auction is great," she said with a look that suggested she was dimly aware of my mental turmoil.

"Spending lots of money?" I asked rather lamely, feeling more like a teenager than the fifty-three year old man who was supposed to be running the show.

"Do you see that exercise machine in the right-hand corner? I'm saving up to buy it for my ex for Christmas. I want to picture him running in place, struggling really to keep his head above water, sweating profusely as he gets nowhere. Isn't that a lovely image for an ex? I think it would make a great present, don't you?"

Her attempt at humor went right over my head, but the word "ex" shot through me as if it was a large artillery shell fired from a cannon. I struggled to recover without giving myself away and blowing the whole thing. "Have you had lunch?" I finally managed to ask, ignoring her question. "It's like Vegas around here. We provide lunch for our best customers."

"That would really be nice," she said with a soft expression that highlighted those wonderful blue eyes. "I read the menu from your sign a while back. I would love a turkey sandwich and a diet Coke."

"Be right back," I said as I left the chair and headed for the lunch counter. There I met Patty Jackson, one of Karen's volunteers and a psychologist at the Valle Crucis School. I placed an order with her for a turkey sandwich, two hot dogs, a Coke and a diet Coke.

"Got a luncheon date?" she rather coyly inquired as she handed me a few dollars change from my ten-dollar bill. Valle Crucis is the kind of place where it's hard to get away with a thing.

"I'm not sure what I have," I smiled back at her. "She's obviously a visitor. Pretty, don't you think?"

"Quite," she responded, handing me the hot dogs. "Good luck."

"Thanks," I replied as I arranged the lunch on a tray and started walking back to where the woman was located on the right side near the wall.

Being off to the side was a good place to eat lunch because it was possible to place the tray on a table and talk with a little privacy.

"This is great," she said as I placed the tray on the table and sat down to join her. She pulled her chair around toward the table, and we were both staring directly at the wall.

"Not much atmosphere," I laughed as I turned to face her.

"Well, at least there's a window not far from us. This will do just fine. By the way, my name is Abby Dunbar, and you must be Jeff, am I correct?"

"Right. It's nice to finally meet you. Are you here to see the leaves?"

"Yes, though technically I'm at an academic convention. I teach in the honors program at Chapel Hill. I'm attending the Association of Integrative Studies meeting at the Broyhill Center."

"Sounds interesting," I said, sipping my Coke. "Are you there to give a paper?"

"No, just to learn. The honors program I teach in is interdisciplinary," she said, picking up a section of her sandwich.

"You mean how Shakespeare relates to economics and why science is really an art form?"

"Exactly. We meet through Wednesday, and then I plan to spend the rest of the week nosing around your area. The convention is perfectly planned. Fall break is next Thursday and Friday. That gives me a legitimate excuse to be away for a whole week." Damn, I thought. She'll be here for an entire week, and my hopes soared. I was becoming quite interested in seeing this woman again.

"Will you be able to use any of these books for your classes?" I asked while directing my gaze at the open box on the floor.

"Not unless I teach a course in Russian literature, but the books are classics. I read most of them in graduate school," she said as she reached down into the box and pulled out a book. It had a thick black cover and a decidedly weathered look. "*Dead Souls*, by Nikolay Gogol. Have you ever heard of it?"

"No, I don't think so," I said, picking up the second hot dog and preparing to lift it to my mouth. But the title shook me a little, and caused me to stop. It was as if the book was about my recent past which I had worked so hard to put behind me. My new story would be called Resurrected Soul, I concluded as I returned my focus to the hotdog. It tasted amazingly good, and I felt better now that my little anxiety attack was over.

"Gogol was this timid little man from the Ukraine. He wrote really funny stories that feature strange characters. *Dead Souls* is about a con man who purchases records of dead people for a money making scheme."

"Sounds quite contemporary. When did the guy write it?"

"All these books come from the incredible 19th century. It is the crowning glory of Russian literature. I would love to meet the person who brought the books here," she said, returning *Dead Souls* to the box.

"If it had been a larger gift, the donor's name would have been written on one of our fact sheets which describes each item. But with things like this, people often just come by in the morning and leave it here. So the books could have come from several people. We live in an interesting community. There are lots of people with money who have second homes. The natives include artists, builders, and teachers, people who work in the ski industry, a few high-powered business executives, and organic farmers. You name it. The place has an interesting mix."

"Sounds like it," she said with a soft smile that spread across a face that exuded enthusiasm and a quiet, gentle energy. "Tell me a little about your work. I gathered from your introduction this morning that you're the guy in charge."

"I take care of the Park which involves about thirty hours of landscape work each week. I love being outdoors. The rest of my job includes fundraising and assisting our volunteers. Recently I've been spending a lot of time with the nature conservancy part of the organization. It's new, and I've enjoyed helping a few dedicated Board members with a real interest in preserving our precious valley set it up."

"You're involved in all kinds of worthwhile endeavors. I'm impressed," she said as she looked over at me and smiled. I thought I detected a little interest in the tone of her voice. Hope surged through me for a second time.

"Thanks. The best part of the job is working with our little community. The people are so appreciative of all I do, much of it undeserved I might add, and they are more than willing to pitch in when I need help. Today is a good example of what I mean. I am the only paid employee, so all the other people you see working here are volunteers."

"I'll have to come back to Valle Crucis and explore the area more thoroughly when the meetings wind up on Wednesday," she said as she put the remains of our lunch back on the tray.

"Do you like to walk?" I asked as I slowly slid my chair from under the table. I wanted desperately to have her pull another book from that box so our conversation could continue. But I had to get back to work. It was a horrible thought.

"It's one of my most favorite things to do," she said, smiling back at me.

"You'll have to come back and walk in our Park then. There's no prettier place in the world to walk."

"Is it close by? I would love to get a little exercise before returning to the Broyhill."

"It's right down the road—less than half a mile from here. What are your plans for the rest of the afternoon?"

"Well, I think I've had enough of the auction, although I don't really have plans. Are you free to walk with me?" My heart jumped. I had never hated my job till that very moment.

"Unfortunately, I'm tied up here for the rest of the afternoon, but if you're ready to leave, let me carry your books to the car and point you in the right direction to the Park."

"That would be great. Please let me pay for the lunch. I know it all goes for a good cause," she gently pleaded as she rose from the chair.

"Not today," I said as I got up with her. "However, I will give you one of our brochures which describes our little organization. We live on contributions."

"I would be happy to give," she said while turning to face the exit at the back of the room. "Before I leave, I do have one additional favor to ask. Can you point me in the direction of the ladies' room?"

"Sure," I said, lightly putting my right hand on her shoulder. "Unfortunately, you're headed the wrong way." And I gently turned her in the other direction. "Go out these double doors beyond the stage and turn left. You'll see it about twenty yards down the hall on the left. When you're finished, you need not come back through this room. Just wander outside, and I'll meet you there with the books."

On the way back to return the tray, I met my friend Peter Hathaway at the food booth. Peter is the owner of the Mast Store, and a fixture in the community. He and his wife Marty bend over backwards to help the Park, as was evidenced today in their loaning us their truck. "Have a nice lunch?" Peter asked with a knowing wink. Peter was about my age, maybe a little younger and an avid walker himself. He would often join me at the Park after work for a brief walk and some stimulating conversation.

"It went much too quickly," I responded as I handed the tray to Karen. She looked beat.

"Good luck, old buddy."

"Thanks, Peter," I responded with a smile. "As you well know, it's been a long time." I looked back toward Karen to thank her for all that she'd done and to reassure her that it wouldn't be long now, but she was emptying the tray and so I left to gather the books.

It didn't take Abby long to meet me. She was taller than I had thought, maybe 5'8", and she was thin with an athletic figure. All the women in my life were constructed that way. Maybe that was a good omen. I still had no idea how old she was; but she must be at least forty, I thought as I watched her walk the last few steps along the corridor before arriving at the double doors. It was her professional manner that suggested she was in her early forties, and yet she had a youthful, energetic look that was so appealing. She smiled at me as she joined me on the steps, and we headed toward the courtyard together. "My car is parked to the left along the street."

"You must have gotten here early. That's a prime spot."

"About 8:30, maybe a little before. I like to get to auctions early so I can look at things before the bidding starts," she said as she led the way toward her car, a 1995 white Toyota Camry station wagon.

"But you didn't buy much," I replied. "Only these books."

"I was often tempted, but then I would have to get the stuff back to Durham next Sunday."

"Is Durham where you live?"

"Yes, do you know it?"

"I've been there a few times. My son was a student at Duke."

"It's a great school. You must be proud of him."

"I am. Durham is a nice place."

" Actually, we live between Durham and Chapel Hill. I have a twenty-minute commute to school. It couldn't be better," she said as she opened the back door to the Camry.

As I loaded the books into the back seat, I asked for a recommendation. Anything to keep the conversation going a little longer. "Is there a book here I might enjoy reading?" I asked as I closed the door.

"I'd be happy to give you Tolstoy's *War and Peace*. I have a copy at home."

"Tolstoy was a Christian pacifist, wasn't he?"

"Yes, he did a good job of taking the glory out of war. He argues in *War and Peace* that peace is best found in the private deeds and thoughts of individual people."

"That's a nice idea, but doesn't the book take forever to read?"

"It does," she said as she started to walk toward the front of the car. "I'm afraid you'd find much of the novel rather boring, particularly the first hundred pages."

"Then I won't take you up on your offer," I said as I smiled across at her. "Now let's get you to the Park. It couldn't be easier. Turn your car around and go over that little bridge," I said as I directed her gaze by pointing my finger down the road. "The Park driveway is the first one on your left."

"Thanks ever so much," she said as she started to get into the car. "It's been a fun auction."

"One more thing," I said with my heart pounding. I really did feel like a teenager now, and I couldn't believe it was this difficult. The thought flew through my mind that I must be shy or something, but the real problem was that I was way out of practice. It had been thirty-five years since I had popped such a question. I guess that explains the rather awkward manner in which I handled the situation. Why couldn't I be smooth like all those studs that cheat on their wives? And then I just got on with it. "You said you enjoyed walking. Would you be interested in a hike toward the end of the week?"

"That would be lovely," she said as she delayed her entrance into the car. "We finish our meetings after lunch on Wednesday. Wednesday afternoon would be perfect. Is that a good time for you?

"I'm free most of that day.

"Call me at the Broyhill then on Tuesday night."

"Abby Dunbar, right?"

"That's me. I look forward to your call," she said as she climbed into the driver's seat.

"Enjoy the meetings," I said in a loud voice which she probably was unable to hear. My heart was still pounding as I waited for her to turn the car around. When she came up to me again, she rolled down the window.

"Sure I can't talk you into walking with me at your park?"

"No, I better wait till Wednesday."

"See you then," she said; and she was gone, moving slowly down the road and across the bridge.

As I waved goodbye, it suddenly occurred to me that I had forgotten to give her the brochure. Oh well, that can wait till Wednesday too, I thought as I turned back toward the school. Then the rest of my afternoon flashed before me. The cafeteria had to be cleaned, the money counted, the unsold goods loaded back into the truck and then unloaded at the Mast Store warehouse, and I rapidly descended to Planet Earth. It would be 6 p.m. before my day was finally over.

Unfortunately, Sunday didn't look much better. I would spend much of the day writing thank you notes to the volunteers who had helped out in some way. Thank you notes were an important part of my job, and I never looked forward to writing them. It wasn't that they took a long time to write. The problem was getting started. Sunday had to be the day. The worst thing was to let them hang over your head.

But that was all in the future. At that moment, my step was light as I walked back to the auction. I had a woman in my life, or at least it was a real possibility, for the first time in a long while. I paused briefly in the courtyard and thought how much fun it would be to be playing my guitar in this beautiful fall weather under the changing maple tree in front of the main school building. And then I got real. Where I really wanted to be was in that car with that enchanting woman with the Russian literature books. But Wednesday would be here before long, and so I smiled as I reentered the school building through those same double metal doors.

Chapter 5

Boone Fork Trail

LIFE IS STRANGE, I thought as I drove to work on Monday morning. It is filled with twists and turns, with roads taken and not taken, with doors that open and those that slam shut. I was thankful that my doors seemed to be opening. The last twelve months, especially, had been good ones. I was moving out of the shade created by my inner shadow, that dark undercurrent of personality that does so much damage when not properly understood, into a bright and exciting light. I greeted this new day with a grateful heart.

I was pleased that my divorce had gone smoothly and that Rebecca, from all that I had heard from Brenda, was really blossoming. She had used her share of the mutual fund money to buy a little house. She continued with her job as organist and choir director at the church and was now teaching music lessons to supplement her income. I'm not sure whether she was dating yet. I somehow find it difficult to think of her as a sexual being, but maybe that too will come with time. I was excited that my share of the money, which I had not yet touched, was doing well. It was a function of the amazing stock market of the nineties. I had no idea how I would eventually use the money, and I knew that historically stocks go up and down, but for now I was content to leave it invested and ride with the winnings. That was also how I intended to live my new life.

I was also pleased that the Park was making progress with the nature conservancy and that I had a second job. Peter Hathaway had tipped me off about the Woodlands job. Peter and the owner of Woodlands, an authentic barbecue restaurant in Blowing Rock, were friends at Rotary. Woodlands was looking for a second entertainer to play three nights a week. I was thrilled to be performing on stage, a new gig for me, and the extra money provided me with a mind-easing cushion.

Most importantly with regard to my work, I was thankful for my new attitude toward it. Slowly, I was learning to work to please myself. The need to impress others was diminishing. I had successfully buried it. I was better able to say no to people. I was shedding the mask that had always wanted to be all things to all people, and I felt that my life was gaining a new authenticity that it had previously lacked. I wasn't exactly sure where I was headed, but I was confident that greater clarity would come with time.

In addition, I was thankful for Brenda. She kept coming back to visit which, as you can imagine, was a great lift to my spirits. I felt a twinge of selfish jealousy about her upcoming marriage, but I knew that in time my heart would expand to share her. I certainly liked Hank and was proud of the fact that the two of them had landed good jobs after completing their graduate studies.

Finally, I thought as I stopped my car at the split rail fence that formed the boundary of the Park's parking lot, I was thankful for October. October was wrap-up month for landscaping at the Park, and I was looking forward to a reduction in schedule. The grass usually only required two cuttings in October before a series of heavy frosts ended the growing season for the year. My project for the next two days was to complete as much of that landscape work as possible. This involved cutting seven acres of playing fields and open spaces with my little red Toro tractor. There were several places that required hand mowing, and some shrubs to trim along the Watauga River.

If the truth be known, this part of my job was hard to call work. The weather couldn't have been better for this time of year. October is usually a dry month in the mountains and warm enough so that the outdoors can still be enjoyed. I had earphones and musical tapes to keep my mind occupied while riding the tractor. It was a good way to add to my repertoire for Woodlands. I also enjoyed seeing friends and neighbors on the walking trail while working. That gave me an opportunity to break the monotony of mowing by stopping to chat or even to take a lap or two if my cramped legs needed stretching.

By late Tuesday afternoon, things at the Park were in pretty good shape. So were my plans for Wednesday. I had called Abby when I got home from work on Tuesday and was lucky to get her in her room. She had never heard of the Boone Fork Trail, but when I told her that it was just off the

Blue Ridge Parkway in Blowing Rock, she sounded excited. She said she would be ready at 1:30 p.m.

Wednesday morning was an easy one. I prepared September's financial statement, which involved placing recent check entries into the computer and pushing a button, and the agenda for the Board meeting scheduled for next Monday evening. I also worked on two new songs for Woodlands. After finishing a light lunch at 12 noon, there was nothing to do but wait. I became anxious about the hike for the first time since asking her on Saturday. It was my first date, if that is the proper name for a walk in the woods with a woman, since leaving Rebecca and Massachusetts three and a half years ago, and I wondered why I had waited so long. I hoped it would go well. She seemed like an extraordinary woman at the auction. I tried to picture her face and remembered only the soft blue eyes, the short black hair, and the engaging smile. Some of the details of that pretty face were lost from my mind, but it wouldn't be long before the real thing would bring it all back.

I finally set off for Boone at 12:45 in my blue 1992 Subaru station wagon. Too bad I wasn't free tonight, I thought as I pulled out of the driveway. Greg Williamson had asked me over for dinner. It sounded like he wanted to discuss some problem at the church with his "objective friend," and so I'd better go. I also had to work at Woodlands on Thursday night. Damn, I thought. I spend most of my nights home alone, and I'm busy the last two nights she's here. At least I have this afternoon I thought as I left the gravel road and turned onto George's Gap. I smiled as I passed the Sparkling Creek Missionary Baptist Church and thought that it was unlikely I would be visiting my two lady friends at church on Sunday.

I arrived in the lobby of the Broyhill Center, which sits on the crest of most of Appalachian State's campus at 1:25. I spotted Abby immediately. She was sitting on the right side of the lobby reading a magazine. The sound of my approaching steps attracted her attention. She smiled in recognition as I stopped about five feet in front of her and said: "Ready to go hiking?"

"You bet. We couldn't have picked a better afternoon," she said as she placed her magazine on the end table and got up from the sofa.

"You look great," I said feeling a little better about things than I had a few hours back. She was wearing a green turtleneck, blue sweatshirt with a white Durham Youth Soccer monogram, jeans, and hiking boots.

"Thanks," she said. "Do you think I'll need this vest?"

"Take it," I answered. "You can always leave it in the car if it feels warm at Price Park."

"Okay," she replied as she picked up the red plaid vest from the sofa. "That's a good idea. At least it saves me a trip back to the room." We walked together through the lobby and the doors that led outside. As we turned left and headed for my car in the parking lot, she faced toward me and asked, "How did things go at the auction?"

"Great. I think when the final figures are in we will net more than $14,000, which is a record."

"Good for you. Let me add a little to that. I left without paying for those books," she said as she reached into her pocket and handed me a check.

"Wow! That's a lot more than the cost of those books."

"I was really impressed with your park and enjoyed my walk on Saturday. Now instead of sending me a brochure, you can write me a thank you note. I would much prefer receiving that."

"You've got a deal," I said as I placed the check in my back pocket.

"I tried to talk a colleague into walking with me there yesterday afternoon, but we were a little pressed for time so we decided to go to the Greenway instead. We had just gotten back when you called."

"That's another lovely walking trail," I said as I opened the front door of the car for her. She climbed into the seat and acknowledged her thanks with a smile. "I've been looking forward to this hike all week," I said as I climbed into the seat beside her. "It's about five miles. Shouldn't take us more than two hours—maybe a little less. Depends on how many times we stop."

"Sounds wonderful," she replied. "I'm in no hurry to get back. I haven't any plans for tonight." And a wave of disappointment passed through me. It's too bad Greg is such a good friend, I thought as I eased the car out of the parking space and headed for Blowing Rock.

*　　*　　*

Boone Fork Trail is located near Blowing Rock, a quaint little mountain town on the southern end of Watauga County. Blowing Rock has a few unique tourist attractions, and many, many shops. It is a place that has been discovered by both tourists and those seeking a second home in the mountains. It was precisely this kind of development that the Board members of the Valle Crucis Community Park were seeking to avoid when they voted to add the nature conservancy function to our organization.

The actual trail is located a few miles south of Blowing Rock just off the Blue Ridge Parkway in Julian Price Memorial Park. The drive from the Broyhill Center took twenty minutes. On the way there, I asked Abby about her morning meetings. She was animated about the first session on the political novel. The presenter was an American literature specialist, but all Abby could talk about were those Russian books. "All Russian literature in the nineteenth century was political," she commented with enthusiasm as she looked over at me. "It would make for a great course at Chapel Hill. I'm sure it would take a year or two to prepare, but new courses are what keep me alive academically." She exalted at her good fortune at being at the auction, and I thanked God for the first time in many years.

We left the car at the parking lot at Price Park, walked side by side across an open field, crossed a small bridge and entered onto the trail. The trail is perfect for this kind of hike, a short outing, because it is circular. Five miles later it would bring us back to this same spot. Because the trail is narrow, I led the way as the trail descended rather steeply downhill. Soon we were climbing down over large rocks and the stump of an old oak tree. I looked back at Abby, who smiled to say that everything was fine. She navigated the tree stump with the grace of a deer leaping over a short fence.

After the first ten minutes, the trail leveled out, so I picked up the pace. The river, I apologize for not being able to remember its name, was clearly visible on the right, which added to the appeal of the hike. Another alluring phenomenon was a rhododendron canopy which provided a thick, thatched roof over the trail for ten yards or more. As I exited from under the canopy, my mind began to imagine royal gardens and a palace when suddenly Abby whispered, "Jeff, come back here." I stopped and turned to face her, and she put her finger to her lips. I quietly retraced the five yards that separated us, and she gently placed her right arm across my shoulder and turned me so that I was facing the woods.

"A pileated woodpecker. Do you see it?" she whispered.

"Not yet," I replied, and then she pointed her left hand and steered my focus a little to the left and upwards.

"It's perched on the limb of that old oak tree. About thirty feet up."

"Oh, yeah. I see it. How do you know it's a pileated woodpecker?"

"Because of the red crest, and the black and white striped face," she whispered back.

"It's impressive," I said, and she gently squeezed my shoulder before dropping her arm. Sparks surged through me. Then she teased: "You men always have some goal in mind. We're not out to break a world speed record. You'll miss all the good stuff if you keep at your present pace."

"Sorry. My mind was distracted with royal gardens and palaces," I said as I turned away from the woodpecker to face her.

"Well, at least you have some imagination," she responded as she smiled up at me. "I've never seen rhododendron bushes arranged that way."

"Canopies like that are all over mountain trails around here," I said as the woodpecker took off and flew over the trail and above our heads.

"We'll see another," Abby said as she watched him fly away.

"I'll keep the pace down. Sorry about that! There is a large rock in the river a few minutes from here. I always enjoy sitting on it and looking around."

"Sounds like a good stopping point. Don't worry about the pace. I was only kidding. I can always keep up. I just wanted you to see that woodpecker."

*   *   *

We arrived at the rock in the river about fifteen minutes later. It was a little farther ahead on the trail than I had remembered. It is a flat rock, where the river bends around a corner and widens, that juts out about eight feet into the water. I stepped onto it, extended a hand for Abby, and gently pulled her up. She walked the few steps toward the center of the rock and turned in a 360-degree circle. "This spot is so beautiful, Jeff. Look at the sun on that water."

"I like to sit here, close my eyes, and listen to the river as the water gurgles its way downstream." Sit I did, but my eyes remained riveted on her, devouring her really, as she continued to survey the scene around the rock. She was thin, but with breasts just large enough to make her figure very exciting. I was thinking again about her age, it was a puzzle that I was hung up on, when she nailed me.

"A penny for your thoughts," she said with a broad grin that suggested she knew exactly what had been running through my mind these last few moments.

As she sat down beside me, I responded, "Whoops. I was just thinking how right you are about the water."

"You can't see the water from that position," she replied with the same grin on her face.

"So I guess you want a better answer."

"That would be nice."

"I was looking for gray hairs."

"Melanie Jakoe."

"Melanie Jakoe?" I repeated.

"Yes. My hairdresser."

"Oh, so you cheat a little. That makes me feel a whole lot better."

"I didn't say that. I just said I had a hairdresser. Does age matter to you?" she asked with a grin that acknowledged she had the upper hand.

"Not really. I'm just trying to guess, and I keep coming up ten years apart with my guesses."

"I like the mystery. It's good to be a little mysterious, don't you think?" she said with a wink.

"Is mystery part of feminine power?" I asked, returning her grin.

"Absolutely," she smiled back.

"What then is masculine power? How would you define it?"

"Quietly," she responded.

"That's wonderful," I laughed.

She smiled back, and placed her hand on my knee. She was making me weak. "Tell me about your conservancy?" she inquired after a brief pause in the conversation. I felt relieved that she changed the topic. It had been fun, and it had also gone far enough.

"Right now we're just getting started. We recently got together a committee of ten people to devise a strategy to preserve the rural character of Valle Crucis. The idea would be to purchase land and conservation easements to protect the area from adverse development."

"Explain to me what a conservation easement is. I have heard the term before, but I really don't have a clear idea what one is."

"It's an agreement that limits the future development of a piece of property. For example, you pay a farmer a sum of money in exchange for his signing a document which says that future buyers of the property may not divide the land into smaller parcels. The contract remains in force forever."

"Sounds like a good conservation tool."

"It is because you avoid the full cost of buying the property and at the same time you accomplish your conservation goal."

"What's your role with the conservancy?"

"I've got to raise the money to pay for the Board's dreams."

"Are you good at picking people's pockets?"

"We'll see. I've done this sort of thing all of my professional life, but the fundraising base of Valle Crucis is small. That makes it an interesting challenge."

"I'm sure it is," she reflected as she took her hand off my knee, placed it on the rock and along with her other hand, pushed herself up. She scanned the area one more time, looked down at me and said, "It really is beautiful. Thanks so much for bringing me here."

"Are you ready to go?" I asked, holding my hands up for assistance.

"You better get up yourself," she said. "I don't want to end up in the water."

"I thought women had power," I pleaded.

"Mystery," she said as she jumped off the rock and headed down the trail. She led the way for the next forty-five minutes. The trail wound around a magnificent cliff where a huge gray rock face looked like the bow of a navy destroyer. It also crossed back and forth across the river. At one point the bridge was nothing more than a series of stepping-stones. Abby waited for me half way across the stream and offered her hand, laughing all the while. When I turned her down, she skipped across the remaining stones and darted ahead. She moved with the light step of a ballet dancer, and I hurried to match her pace.

Then I thought about the big meadow. It shouldn't be more than twenty minutes from here. It was another great place to stop, and I worried about Scott. I was sure we would talk about our children at some point. It was both natural and inevitable. What would I say about him? It bothered me that I was not quite over Scott after four years. The wound had healed; but there was a scab over it, a scab that wouldn't flake off and that I was terrified to pick at. I was afraid that if I disturbed the scab, it would only open up the wound and I would bleed again. My train of thought was broken as I approached two large boulders with a stepladder between them that had to be negotiated. Abby had stopped there to wait for me. "This is such an interesting trail, Jeff," she said with a smile. "You doin' okay?"

"Fine. You look like you do this sort of thing every day. I'm impressed with your stamina."

"I have a Nordic Track."

"You must use it often."

"No, but I do manage to dust it once a month. Now, what do you suggest we do here? Do you want to go first?" she asked with a wide grin.

"No. You're really doing well." As I stood there chuckling, it occurred to me in a quick flash of intuition that she appreciated my allowing her to lead. I never worried about such things. I was just grateful for being in the presence of a strong woman, a woman who balanced feminine warmth and grace with an independence and self-confidence I admired. "Just work your way up and around on the ladder."

"I wish the trail was wide enough to go side by side," she said as she moved closer to the first large rock and the rope stepladder.

"The last twenty minutes is good for that," I said while watching her start up the ladder. "Be careful on that ladder," and she looked up at me with a grin that said no problem. "There's a large meadow about fifteen minutes ahead. You can wait for me there."

"You won't be far behind, will you?"

"Not unless I get delayed watching a woodpecker," I said with a laugh.

"Just remember its name and markings," she said, smiling back at me and then refocusing her concentration on the ladder as she took another step toward the top of the rock.

* * *

The meadow is three or four acres of carpeted grassland with Grandfather Mountain in the background. As I came out from the narrow-wooded path, I joined Abby and said: "How about we take a short breather by that sugar maple over there?" The sugar maple stood alone in the open pasture with leaves that were in the early stages of change. Soon it would be crimson red, a sight that would be worth coming back for.

"I'm ready," she replied smiling. "This place is the best!" she commented softly, as if to herself, as she looked across the meadow. Her scan of the area quickly halted as her attention was directed down a small hill and over to a pool of water. "Oh, look at those cows over on the left. Are we on some farmer's land?"

"You know, I'm not really sure. I've never seen cows here before."

"I guess that wooden fence marks off the property," she said as we walked together toward the sugar maple. We sat next to each other with our backs against the tree, facing Grandfather Mountain and the slowly fading sun.

"That's Grandfather over there, isn't it?" she asked as she moved herself into a new position to get comfortable.

"Sure is," I answered.

"Such a captivating sight."

"It's one of the biggest tourist attractions in North Carolina," I said as I moved closer to her. "What an incredible face God carved out of those rocks—the beard, chin, nose, eye sockets." And as I looked across at her, I wondered whose incredible face I was envisioning.

"I suppose it took a long time for her to finish the project."

"Yes, but God's time is not like ours," I said, shifting my focus and looking over at Grandfather.

"True, but sitting here with no deadlines, looking out at this peaceful scene, helps to narrow the difference."

"A window into eternity," I said as I stretched my legs and leaned farther back against the tree. We were comfortably quiet for several moments, when Abby gently rested her head on my shoulder and asked:

"Tell me about your family, Jeff? I assume you haven't lived alone all your life."

"I was married for twenty-six years—more than a quarter of a century. That's a long time. Our divorce was finalized last year."

"Was it amiable?"

"Just very sad. It was sad because we never tried to work out our differences. It was also sad because we had such a long, common history, and I know we would have enjoyed being grandparents together. But she was probably right. By the time I left Massachusetts in the spring of '95 we had so little in common a reconciliation would have been difficult if not impossible. She was just so angry at me."

"Then you have children," Abby responded. I was a little relieved she didn't probe the subject of the angry wife, and yet here we were talking about our children.

"We had children, and now we have a child," I answered in a quiet voice as if to myself. "Brenda, our oldest, is twenty-seven, and living in Newton, Massachusetts with her soon to be husband. She is teaching school there, and Hank has a job with a large Boston law firm. They plan to get married over Memorial Day weekend."

"Sounds like they're in pretty good shape," she said as she patted my knee with her left hand. After a brief pause, she continued, "Do you mind if I ask if there was another child? Did you lose one?"

I looked off in the distance and replied after a brief pause. "Yes, we had a son named Scott. He died in a bicycle accident in Charleston four years ago." And then I had to smile a little inside, which helped to hold back the tears. I hadn't talked to anyone about Scott, except Brenda, since leaving Massachusetts, and here I was spilling it out to a woman I hardly knew. Female mystery, I thought, as I gained more confidence.

"That's really sad," she commented as she took my hand and gently squeezed it. "Do you want to talk about him?"

"I'm not sure. I've been wondering about it since we started hiking. Part of me says no, but my clinical training suggests it would be a good idea. He had gone down to see his girlfriend at the College of Charleston in May after exams. She was showing him the city on their bikes. I'm sure he was showing off or just riding with little concern for his safety."

"That's what scares me about kids. They never think anything bad can happen to them," she interjected.

"You're right, but it did. Evidently, he turned a corner without looking and ran head on into this guy who was driving a furniture truck. At least there was no suffering. He died before the ambulance reached the scene."

"So he was in college?" And she paused briefly, "Oh yes, he was the one at Duke."

"He had just finished his freshman year. Starting wide receiver on the football team. It was quite an achievement."

"I would say so. You must have been very proud of him. I know Duke well. I've got some friends who teach there. It's a great school—both in football and academically."

"The thing that made him so special was his remarkable combination of talents. He was trying to decide whether to major in music or physics. He had taken piano lessons from his mother since he was six, and he also loved ballet." And then I smiled a second time. "The coach from the University of Illinois wanted to sign him; but he told Scott the long hair had to go. Scott politely said, No thank you."

"He sounds like a very interesting young man," she said in a tone of great warmth.

Now that I had started I wanted to continue. It felt so good talking about Scott this way. It wasn't as if she had ripped open the scab, but rather she had opened a space in my heart that was still crying out to be honored. Brenda's interest had created a similar effect. Women have the most wonderful instincts about these things, I thought to myself before charging on. "He got me to my first ballet recital."

"Was it fun?"

"I enjoyed those recitals as much as the football games."

"Good for you."

"So did many of his teammates. There were thirty or more present for his senior recital. In many ways, he was much more like his mother than me—so earnest and goal oriented. In high school he wouldn't talk with his friends at night until his homework was done. He was also a prominent member of the Fellowship of Christian Athletes. I wish he was here today so we could go drinking together. I need his companionship, and he needed to loosen up."

"Did you ever go drinking with him?" she asked, releasing my hand and shifting her weight.

"No, but I do with Brenda. She and I are soul mates. I don't know what I would have done without her these last three years."

"Do you see her often?"

"She tries to visit me twice a year, though that may be a little more difficult when she gets married. She loves these mountains. We also chat on the phone regularly. She's got it all together. I think you would like her." And I smiled inside as I considered the similarities of the two women. They were both irreverent, for Brenda that was her way of surviving being a minister's daughter, and they both were full of enthusiasm and energy. Maybe that was why I was attracted to Abby, in addition, of course, to those enchanting blue eyes and the thin, athletic figure. We were quiet for some time, just enjoying the setting sun and the amazing surroundings, with her head resting on my shoulder. Finally, I broke the ice. "Now tell me about your children. Do you have any?"

"Yes. Twin girls. Tara and Ana. They're thirteen now. Two teenage girls. Oh, my God, sometimes…."

"They sound fun already. I love their names."

"We chose carefully. My ex is from India. We wanted names that reflected both cultures."

"Interesting. You chose well. Twins have always fascinated me. Are they much alike?"

"They look identical. They have the same brown hair and brown eyes as their father. It would take you awhile to be able to tell them apart. But they have very different personalities. Tara is the more outgoing and athletic one. Ana is more sensitive and into school."

"Are they best friends?"

"Not really, though many of their school friends are the same. They do have a funny sense of dependency, though. Not long after we were divorced, Ana was obviously having a nightmare and so she ran into bed with me. Half an hour later I heard this thud from their bedroom. Tara had fallen out of bed and came crying into my room. 'She's supposed to stop me from doin' that, Mama. Make her get back into bed.' is what Tara wailed, or something close to it. Tara was a restless sleeper, and Ana's body acted as her safety bar. When I suggested that Tara join the two of us in my bed, that ended it."

"That's a good story. I've always heard that about twins. Has the divorce been hard on them?"

"Not really. They have a great father who adores them, and we have become friends again. We live only a few miles apart so the girls go back and forth. It's nice this week cuz they are with him. The divorce was hard on me, though. He had an affair and that was it, but I hurt for a long time. I still loved him when the whole thing blew up."

"But life is good now?"

"Very good. Time has helped a lot in that department."

"That's wonderful. Unless you have been through a divorce, you have no idea what it is like."

"I forgave him for the twins and so I could heal."

"Wow, I'm really impressed," I said as I slowly moved away from the tree and got up on my feet. "Maybe you should counsel Rebecca on forgiveness," I mumbled, mostly to myself.

"Rebecca?"

"My ex. I'm sure she's still loving the fact that she hates me."

"That just hurts her, not you."

"You're so right, and I'm not really sure why I should care or worry about it. Maybe she has forgiven me, who knows. Anyway, now that we have spilled our separate soap operas, I'm afraid we better head for the parking lot. It's 4:45. I guess I told you I have a dinner engagement tonight I better keep," and I offered her a hand to help her up. I kept holding her hand as we started to walk across the meadow.

"That's okay," she said. "How about tomorrow? Do you have some free time then?"

"Till about 5:30 in the evening. Unfortunately, I have a weekly engagement every Thursday night, but that would still give us plenty of time for another hike."

"What I'd really love to do is see those Fresco churches. Have you ever been there?"

"Once. They're in Ashe County, about forty-five minutes from the Broyhill Center."

"Let's go there," she said as she turned toward me with those enchanting eyes shining. "That will make a great last day for me. Unfortunately, I need to pick up the twins on Friday afternoon."

"I know a great place to have lunch. We could make a day of it."

"Sounds exciting," she said as she smiled up at me and gave my hand a slight squeeze. "Can I do anything about lunch? What should I wear?"

"No, leave lunch to me. I'll pick up some sandwiches on my way to the Broyhill. We'll hike to lunch. So just wear what you have on today."

"Sounds easy. Are you sure I can't get lunch?"

"Is Subway okay?"

"Fine. Just get me half a turkey sandwich with everything on it. Ask them to go easy on the mayo if you happen to remember."

"We should be on the road by about 9:30."

"Nine thirty's perfect," she said as we entered the paved area of the trail which circles the campsite. I continued to hold her hand for the fifteen-minute walk to the parking lot. The trip back to Boone was mostly quiet, although I took a slightly different route and pointed out the interesting sights along the way. As I pulled up the car to the front entrance of the Broyhill, we both got out and I walked around to say goodbye. We hugged briefly, but neither of us held back. I squeezed tightly as sparks again ignited inside me.

"Thanks for a lovely afternoon, Jeff," she said as she disengaged herself from me and turned toward the hotel entrance.

"See you tomorrow," I said with a smile as I watched her proceed up the steps.

"Looking forward to it," she grinned back at me as the doors mechanically opened. And with that, nothing remained to be done except to walk around to the front door of my car and proceed home with a mind that was churning on overdrive and a heart that was beating to a new drum.

Chapter 6

Mount Jefferson

FALL IN THE MOUNTAINS of North Carolina is a special time of year. With the rich variety of hardwoods, the color is spectacular, the vegetation lush and green. The air is typically cool and brisk, creating energy and an elan for life that touches even the most damaged soul. It's a time of year when the outdoors screams to be lived in, to be honored, to be enjoyed.

As I closed the door to my little house that Thursday morning and looked across the rolling fields that stood before me, I became caught up in that wonderful spirit of fall. It felt so good to be alive, and I had a full day ahead with Abby Dunbar, which added to my sense of well-being and eager anticipation of what the day might bring. I started my car for the trip to Boone, sensing its power, and a feeling of reckless abandon came over me that had been absent from my life for thirty-five years. I had spent so much time preparing to live and coping with life. Now was the time to just do it. That feeling stayed with me until I encountered the first switchback on Sweetwater Lane, and I was back to being fifty-three again.

I arrived at the Broyhill Center a little before 9:30, and Abby was waiting on the same sofa where I had found her the day before. We hugged briefly in the lobby and then proceeded toward my car. She was full of pleasant chatter about *Stones From the River* by Ursula Hegi. "I'm going to loan it to you when I finish. It's one of the best political novels I have ever read. It takes place in a small town in Germany at the end of World War 1, and it traces the life of Trudi, a dwarf, from 1917 through the take-over of East Germany by the Communists in the late forties. I'm about half way through in the Nazi period. It's fascinating to see how people in a small town responded to the Nazis. Each person reacted differently. Some secretly sheltered Jews, while others turned them in. Many were between those extremes, silent and scared."

"It does sound like my kind of book."

"Her treatment of Trudi is really well done. She is short, not particularly attractive, different from everyone in the town. Yet she shows us by her interactions with a wide variety of people that we are all different in our own unique way."

"I've been learning that about myself in the last few years."

"Good for you. You're way ahead of me. I'll mail you the book as soon as I finish it."

"Keep it at home," I said as I opened the car door for her. "You can give it to me if I'm ever invited to Durham."

"You be a good boy today and get me to those churches, and you have a deal," she said smiling up at me as I closed her door and began the walk to the other side.

As we got underway, she told me about dinner plans she had for this evening. She had an old friend from graduate school days, Judy Larson, who taught constitutional law at ASU. Apparently, they tried to get together at least once whenever Abby was in town. A brief pang of disappointment floated through me when I thought about another lost evening, but I also felt a little better about having to work. Because I was due at Woodlands at 5:30 p.m., I brought my guitar and a change of clothes with me.

The first stop for the morning was Mount Jefferson State Park. Mount Jefferson is in Ashe County, about twenty-five miles north of Boone. The park sits off route 221 and is near the two Fresco churches that Abby was determined to see on this trip. It's an easy forty-five minute drive from Boone through rolling farmland with picturesque barns and little white churches doting the landscape. There are a lot of places around here like the Sparkling Creek Missionary Baptist Church, I thought as I refocused my attention on the two-lane highway.

The road into the state park ends at a picnic area at the top of the mountain. From there an easy hiking trail runs a mile along the summit of Mount Jefferson. My plan was to hike the trail, have lunch at the picnic area, and then visit the Fresco churches.

After parking the car, I walked around to meet Abby and turned her so she was facing in the opposite direction. "Guess what?" I asked.

"Grandfather Mountain," she answered in a voice of real surprise. "It's like we're right back where we started from yesterday, and yet we're much further away. What a view from up here!" With that, I put my arm around her shoulder, squeezed it, and led her through the picnic area and onto the trail.

"The hike is only about a mile, maybe a little more."

"I like it already because we can walk together along the trail," she said as she placed her left arm around my waist.

"That will soon change," I responded as I searched ahead up the trail. As we walked together arm in arm in back of the picnic area, I thought about my first girlfriend in the eighth grade. She had been pretty too and very athletic, that's what we had in common, and she possessed a self-confidence which I definitely lacked. I remembered feeling awkward around her, a little insecure, which led me to overreact, to be dramatic, to want to impress her. I would also make a list of topics for conversation every time I called her. I didn't think I would need such a list with Abby, but I smiled inwardly at the thought that some things never change. The awkwardness was back, but being able to reflect on it was a hopeful sign.

"Look at these hardwoods," she said a few minutes later as she stopped and fixed her gaze slightly to the right and into the woods. "There's a red oak across from us and a sugar maple off to the left just like the one we sat under yesterday. The leaves are close to full color. This is so beautiful, Jeff. I can't even believe I'm here."

"I guess it helps we're a little higher up and further north than yesterday. Do you see the gnarly look of the bark on that red oak? It's fascinating. I wonder what causes that?"

"You've got me," she answered. "It certainly does have a weathered look about it. Maybe it's just old age, a glimpse into our future."

"It's sturdy, though. I'll take wrinkled and sturdy," I said as a soft smile crossed over my face. She took my hand and squeezed it as we resumed our walk together up a gentle slope, and then I took the lead as the gravel trail narrowed into a mountain path. About ten minutes further into the hike, I stopped and turned to face her.

"Do you see those large rocks on the left? I met a guy the last time I was here who claimed runaway slaves would hide in those rocks while they waited to get picked up on the Underground Railroad."

"That's interesting. They're certainly big enough to hide four or five people."

"Want to try it?" I inquired with a grin.

"Not this trip, thanks. I'd hate to know what we'd find in there." With no one else on the trail, at least on this section, and no cars in the parking lot other than my own, I could no longer resist. I moved two steps toward her and put both arms around her. She buried her head between my left shoulder and neck. I held her a few moments, it felt so good, and then she moved her head and looked up at me with eyes that invited me to throw away my innate shyness. We kissed briefly. "I like tall men," she said softly, with eyes that sparkled like frost in the morning when it is touched by a bright sun.

"I like good hikers," I said as I smiled down at her.

"If interest counts, you've got the best," she said as she buried her head into my neck one more time. And then as quickly as it had all started, she separated herself from me and jumped out ahead along the trail with that light gait that reminded me so much of a dancer. I marveled at her playfulness. It made me feel younger. It told me everything was right with the world. I followed after her as the trail leveled off as it continued its course along the summit of Mount Jefferson. She flew by the fork to the left that led to the old fire tower without even seeming to notice.

As I hurried to catch her, I rounded a corner and almost bumped into her. "Oh, Jeff, look at the rotten old stump. I'm sure it's a chestnut, don't you think?"

"It looks like one. What a sad story. When slaves were hiding in the rocks back there, the nuts from this tree were probably a major source of their food. Do you know anything about the horrible blight that attacks these trees? I've often wondered when it hit these parts and how it got here."

"I have no idea," she said as she looked up at me with a somewhat puzzled look on her face. "But life is paradoxical, and I can always find the silver lining. Do you see it here?"

"Yes," I replied with a sense of reverence for the wonder of nature and the essential goodness of life. "I see that little sprouts are coming up. Do you want to know something really special?"

"Yes, tell me something really special," she said as she stooped down to get a closer look at the tiny green shoots.

"You won't believe it when I tell you. There is a retired DNA scientist who has a second home in Valle Crucis. His last assignment before retiring was as a member of a team that is currently developing a spray they hope will cure this blight."

"You're kidding!" she said as she looked up at me.

"Nope. He told me about it last summer. I often walk with him when he comes to the Park. They're testing the spray right now in some lab in Connecticut."

"Valle Crucis is an interesting place," she said as she stood up and looked up the trail. "Your friend may help to save these little sprouts," and then she was off and walking again.

"I hope so," I said, as I started to follow her again.

"Where are we going?" she asked after a few minutes as she looked back over her shoulder.

"Luther's Rock. You'll see the sign momentarily. We're almost there." I kept right behind her, and as we stepped out from the narrow, wooded trail onto a large rock face punctuated with scruffy pine bushes, the whole landscape opened before us. You could see several Christmas tree farms in the distance, a few of the little white churches that had been so evident from the car, and a tiny shopping center. The old fire tower was clearly visible to the left, about a half-mile away along the ridge.

"Do you see that fire tower on the left? You ran right past it a while back."

"What do I want with an old fire tower when I can look at that beautiful river down there," Abby said as she took it all in. "It's so wide and blue. Does the sun always sparkle on mountain streams when you're hiking, Jeff?" she asked as she turned toward me with a warm smile.

"We've been lucky with the weather."

"I guess so, but you pick your spots well."

"I spent my first two months in Watauga County hiking all the trails within a fifty-mile radius of Valle Crucis. So I've come to know the area pretty well."

"It's nice to have a tour guide."

"I'm happy to have a companion."

We were both silent for a while as I placed both arms over her shoulders. She leaned back and snuggled her head up under my neck as my arms gently lay across her breasts with my hands resting on her tummy. I wasn't sure how they had gotten into that position, but I wasn't going to change it no matter how uncomfortable it became. Finally, I broke the silence. "That river out there you like so much is called the New River. It is said to be the oldest river in the world."

That did it. "You're kidding," she said as she shot forward into an upright, standing position to look at the river, which left my hands dangling in space. "Where does it go?" she asked, her gaze fixed forward.

"I think it eventually joins the Ohio which flows into the Mississippi. What you see there is called the South Fork. I'm not exactly sure where the North Fork is, but it's not far from here. The guy who told me about the slave hideout said that the rocks in the riverbed are more than a billion years old."

"That's incredible rocks can be that old. I still can't get over the sparkling blue water," she said as she turned toward me. I put my arms around her waist. As she slowly turned again, about ninety degrees, I moved with her. It was as if we were ice-dancing partners twirling in slow motion. As we gazed in the opposite direction from the river, a large bird came into view. It skirted the edge of the summit in a 180-degree arc.

"Does the hawk come with the tour?" she asked as she took both of my hands.

"How do you know it's a hawk? It just looks like a large bird to me."

"It's a Red-Tailed hawk. Did you see the reddish color of its tail? That's the distinctive mark. They certainly do have mean looking faces. I'm glad I'm not a mouse."

"Me too," I said as I watched the hawk complete its circle and disappear around the bend by the old fire tower. I gently turned Abby toward me, lowered my head and kissed her long and tenderly. I too was soaring like that hawk. As I slowly separated myself from her and came back to earth, Abby smiled up at me and asked:

"Are you getting hungry?"

"Yes, I guess it's about that time. My stomach has a pretty regular clock." I held her hand as we stepped off the rock ledge and then moved on ahead as we started back along the trail. Five minutes later I glanced back at her, and she smiled at me with those playful, dancing blue eyes signaling quite clearly that all was well.

*   *   *

I sat her down at a picnic table in the sun and went to the car to retrieve lunch. I placed the two sandwiches on the table, along with napkins, two plastic cups, and a bottle of red wine which I proceeded to open. "Pretty fancy fare," she said as she watched me at work.

83

"We're on our way to visit some Episcopal churches. This will help us prepare."

"You mean get well tuned."

"Just one glass for me. I'm a light hitter, especially before sundown."

"I bet," she said as she opened the two sandwiches. I poured the wine, took a bite of my roast beef special, and spoke to her, perhaps a little too early, with a mouth that was partially full.

"Tell me about your job. What's it like to be a college professor?"

"I'm not sure there's enough wine here for me to get it all out."

"You mean you're not too wild about teaching?" I persisted.

"No, I didn't quite mean that. Actually, I love my job. For the last nine years I have been teaching part-time in the honor's program. I started at Chapel Hill in 1982 in a tenure track position in the English department. It was a hectic time. There were new classes to prepare and articles to write in hopes of gaining tenure.

"1985 was a really good year. The twins were born, and our economic situation took a giant leap forward, which allowed me to go part-time. The Dean and my department chair were happy to allow me to transfer to the honor's program. I teach two classes on Tuesday and Thursday."

"So you gave up your tenure track position. Was that hard?"

"It was a no brainer. I wanted to be a mother, and I had no interest in publishing."

"Why's that?"

"I wrote my dissertation on *The Red Badge of Courage*. It is a fascinating novel—complex, full of ambiguity. Interpreters see it very differently."

"Did you choose that novel because you grew up in the Vietnam era?"

"That was certainly one of the reasons. My dissertation provided me with three publishable articles, but I kept asking myself so what. What does this prove? Does the world need another article on *The Red Badge of Courage*?"

"I see what you mean."

"But I really do like teaching. I still love to learn, and engaging with students can be fun. We have some good ones."

"I guess so if they are in the honor's program."

"The beauty of that program is that it is interdisciplinary. Excessive specialization is the bane of our existence as academic professionals, at least it was for me. For one thing, it creates a culture of pettiness. When academics get together as a group, they can become petty."

"How so?"

"We are trained to learn so much about so little, to see individual trees and not the whole forest. As practicing professionals, we master a finite body of knowledge for power and self-justification. When we get together on committees, we often don't work well together. The needs of one's discipline take on paramount importance, and the student loses. The issues seem so petty, when looked at from a distance, but the battles can be fierce. Because we know so much about one thing, we think we know about everything. We lack a sense of humility."

"Whoosh. That's a rather harsh indictment," I commented as I took one last sip of wine.

"I know, but you asked for it," she said as she looked over at me rather sheepishly.

"You're right about that. Can you give me an example to clarify what you mean?"

"Sure. I was once a member of the Curriculum Committee. We would meet to decide on academic requirements for the university. The goal, of course, is to require those courses that best suit a student's educational needs. But what so often happens is that decisions are made that have more to do with individual department needs, rather than what is best for the student. We are literally blinded by our narrow-mindedness."

"I see your point," I responded with interest.

"Do you want to know another problem with academic specialization? Boredom! After teaching the same thing over and over again, the material becomes boring. Professors lose interest in their subject and energy in the classroom. The problem is that there is too much work involved, preparation time, in moving into another area. Again, the student is the loser.

"Now before you conclude that I'm the wicked witch from Salem and ditch me right here, let me soften what I've just said."

"I wasn't thinking that at all. In fact, I was impressed with your candor," I said a little defensively. I reached across the table to take her hand, to reassure her that all was well as far as I was concerned.

"That's good, but to be fair one must conclude that individually academics are like everyone else. Some are fine, wonderful people, others are jerks, and many live in between. It's what the environment does to us that I don't like, and I imagine the same thing is true with all professions. Business people as individuals can be decent human beings, but put them in a corporate culture and they can become greedy, cutthroat, and insensitive to anything but the bottom line."

"That's certainly true. Clergy probably operate the same way as a group. But getting back to what you love to do best, I bet your classes are fantastic. I would love to take a course from you. Let me know when you get the Russian lit prepared."

"You just want to sleep with your professor. I've got you all figured out."

"Is that part of the deal?"

"Absolutely not. I'm not for sale."

"Good. I like women with mystery."

"I told you yesterday that was our best gender trait."

"I guess you did. Well, let's go to church and explore another great mystery," I said as I started to gather the paper trash from lunch. She took one last sip of her wine, got up from the table, and came over to hug me.

"Maybe I need a little confessional time after all that venom on academe," she whispered up to me.

"I don't think that's necessary. God still loves you unless he's a lot dumber than I think he is."

"God is not dumb because God is a she. We need to end this he business," she said as she stepped away from me.

"I'll try to keep that in mind."

"That would be nice. You know, I've never thought of myself as a theologian before. Turning God into a feminist will be quite an academic coup."

"I'm afraid there have been others before you."

"As I just said, academic research can be rather tedious."

Chapter 7

The Fresco Churches

WE GOT INTO THE car, headed down the mountain, and turned left onto route 163. It was about a fifteen-minute drive from Mount Jefferson to Holy Trinity Church in Glendale Springs. Instead it took an hour because when we passed the New River, Abby insisted on stopping. She wanted a rock for testing. It was her plan to take a rock from the river to the geology department at her university to see if it was indeed a billion years old.

We stopped along the side of the road and walked about twenty-five yards to the riverbank. A contest between us arose when she insisted I go with her into the middle of the river to get the rock. "No way," I protested. "This is your experiment."

"I don't think so. You put me up to it. You challenged me with that billion-year claim."

"Why not accept it on faith, and we can go to church?"

"Blind faith may be okay in church, but it won't pass muster with science. I want hard proof."

"Then let's walk to the bank, pick up four or five specimens, and that should do it." I wasn't exactly sure how I had gotten myself into this position. I certainly didn't mind a short walk in the river, but she had made a contest out of the whole thing, and I had taken the bait.

"I don't believe this. You're just a big wuss. Now take your boots off and let's get going."

"We're going to freeze in there," I responded as I sat down dutifully and removed my boots. I placed my white wool socks in the boots, and rolled up my jeans to my knees. She was way ahead of me, standing with her feet in the water.

"It's not so bad. I'll even hold your hand," she said as she watched me gingerly approach the water.

"Damn, it's cold," I said as I joined her at the water's edge. "Let's just take our sample from here."

"Not a fair test," she said as she grabbed my hand and started to walk toward the middle of the river. Arriving at what looked to be mid-stream, Abby reached into the water and picked up a rock. She looked it over closely and threw it back.

"What's wrong with that one?" I asked.

"Too round."

"That's the best kind. The roundness tells you it's old. Water running over the surface of that rock over many years has smoothed out the surface."

"You just want to win this little game. You are about to learn I can be a fierce competitor."

"That's what a geologist would tell you."

"Well, I'm not convinced. Let's walk a little further upstream," she said as she led me over more rocks and cold water. It wasn't long before she reached down again and came up with another specimen. "This one's much prettier. See all the spots on it. You hold it, and I'll pick out one more as we walk toward shore."

"What kind will you be looking for this time?"

"One that proves my point."

"Which is?"

"That unfortunately for you, you got stuck with a really silly date."

"I've been convinced of that ever since we left the car. So we can forget about all these crazy rocks."

"But those cute little ankles of yours are turning me on."

"Isn't there an easier way for me to do that?"

"Sure, you can take off your clothes and go for a swim."

"I'll stick to collecting rocks."

"I'm getting better at convincing men to keep their pants on. My daddy would be proud." And then she reached into the water for one more rock. "This should do it," she said, looking over at me with a sheepish grin. "I'm now ready to go to church."

"Be prepared to be on your best behavior."

"That should prove to be a nice change."

*   *   *

With the rock expedition behind us, we proceeded the rest of the way to Holy Trinity without delay. I parked the car in the designated lot, and we walked across the street toward the church grounds which are surrounded by a white picket fence. The church itself is rather small, and definitely quaint in its white paint with light blue trim, and a large steeple. To arrive at the main entrance, it is necessary to skirt an old church graveyard and a rock flower garden, where unfortunately most of the flowers had died from a recent frost.

We entered the church proper through a set of double doors. It was a little spooky because the place was deserted, and yet left wide open for anyone to visit. We felt a little like intruders with Abby looking for someone to sell us admission tickets. Once inside, the quaintness of the place jumps out at you. The interior walls are paneled with natural pine boards, the ceiling is painted white, there are several stained-glass windows along the outside walls which both darken the room and contribute to the general atmosphere of reverence. The altar consists of a simple wooden table. In keeping with the season, this simple table was decorated in a harvest motif. The centerpiece was a hay bale with fruit, vegetables, and several small pumpkins arranged around it with care. A wooden communion rail closes off the sanctuary, and there is a small organ in the back, left hand corner of the church. The sanctuary itself was built to seat about a hundred people.

We walked down the center aisle and sat toward the middle of the sanctuary on the right side. It was the first time I had been in an Episcopal church since leaving Massachusetts three and a half years ago. It was a strange feeling.

As Abby sat down on the wooden pew, it looked as if she wanted to kneel and pray. "This church is both simple and awe inspiring," she said as she finished her initial survey. "The fresco of the Last Supper in front of the altar is beautiful. It's a work of art with real spiritual passion."

"Abby," I asked in a quiet voice that befitted the setting. "I hate to sound dumb, but what is a fresco? I know it's a painting, but what makes it so special?"

"It's special because of the technique developed in ancient Rome. The artist paints on wet or new plaster which allows the pigment from the paint to work its way into the plaster. This helps to preserve the painting, and it gives it a special texture."

"Interesting. The fresco of the Last Supper certainly makes this church a unique place to worship." We were silent for several minutes as we allowed the simple beauty of the surroundings to penetrate us. I put my arm around her, and she snuggled up close. It was a lovely spiritual moment.

But nothing remains constant with Abby Dunbar for long. She broke the silence and asked: "Do you see that door to the left, Jeff? The one that leads to a little room. What's that room called? I can see it asked on a New York Times crossword puzzle."

"That's the sacristy," I replied. "It's where the priest prepares communion, and where the bread and wine are stored. You'll also find linens, crosses, and candles in there."

"I knew it, I knew it, I knew it," she blurted out. The reverent atmosphere of the last ten minutes changed dramatically. I smiled as I wondered what was coming next. I didn't have long to wait. "You were a minister. I had a gut feeling all along you were a professional of some type and this park work was a new venture. You gave yourself away, my dear ex-father, at lunch when you let slip that clergy could be asses too when placed in a group."

"Oh my goodness. I've got myself involved with a smart one. Now that the cat's out of the bag, I can perform communion for you if you like. You said you might be in need of forgiveness at lunch. I'm a little rusty, but I'm sure it will all come back."

"This is really interesting," she said as she looked directly at me with a warm grin and those teasing blue eyes. "Why did you leave? Are you an Episcopalian?"

"So many questions," I said in a tone of bemused exasperation. "Yes, I was an Episcopalian, and why I left is a long story I'd rather leave for another time. I have a copy of my resignation at home. It's all there. You can read it if you ever come to my house."

"Is that a promise?" she asked as she continued to look directly at me.

"Absolutely. I have nothing to hide. I can even put a copy in the mail to you on Friday."

"No need to do that. I would love to see your house if I'm ever invited."

"I think I can manage to do that. Maybe I'll keep the rocks with me so you'll want to return sooner rather than later."

"I'm not sure I want to see those things ever again. Now before we move on to the other church, I want to play a game with the little reverend."

"What's that?" I asked in eager anticipation.

"We'll call it, 'Name that Apostle.' You go first," she said as she looked over at me with a wide grin.

"What do you mean?"

"Okay, I'll go first, and I'll give you an easy one. Who's the person with the beard in the middle of the fresco?"

"Oh, I get the game. That's obviously Jesus, but he wasn't an apostle."

"That's why I asked you first. You don't get a point for that. Now ask me one."

"Who's the guy leaving the door on the upper left?" I asked. I was getting into the game. Her playful spirit was contagious.

"Looks like Judas to me. One zip. Now, who's the guy on the far end of the table with a scroll?"

"Matthew."

Good for you," she said. "We're even at one apiece. I'm waiting."

"Okay, how about the guy next to Jesus scratching his chin?"

"The trouble with this game is they're all guys," she said smiling. "This one's a little tougher." There was silence for a moment, and then she asked. "Can you give me a clue?"

"I would guess him to be Peter because of his position next to Jesus and because of the puzzled look on his face. Remember he was the one who had so much trouble honoring his commitment to Jesus."

"I think you have me there. I never should have played this game with a minister."

"I'll give you a chance to get even."

"To take revenge or to get even. That is the question."

"What would you do to get revenge?"

"Take you back to the river."

"You win."

"That makes me feel a whole lot better. I told you I can be a fierce competitor."

*　　*　　*

The drive to St. Mary's Episcopal Church took another twenty minutes. The church is located near West Jefferson, the principal town in Ashe County. We arrived there about 3:45 in the afternoon, and there were three or four cars in the parking lot as we drove up.

St. Mary's is a little smaller than Holy Trinity, but with the same simple beauty. A similar white picket fence surrounds the church perimeter. The interior of the church is all done in natural wood with strikingly handsome stained-glass windows along each sidewall. In front of the altar, there are three frescos—Jesus on the cross in the center with a pregnant Mary on his left, and John the Baptist to his right.

We visited the Church at St. Mary's more as tourists than a couple on a date. We sat on the right side again toward the back of the church with seven or eight other people scattered in front of us. Because someone had found the appropriate button, we listened to an interesting audio presentation on the frescos. We learned that Ben Long had painted the three frescos in the 1970s, he was also the artist of the Last Supper at Holy Trinity, and that the model for the pregnant Virgin Mary had been a local mountain woman.

At 4:15 p.m. I nudged Abby and whispered that it was time to go. She was ready, and we made a silent exit to the car. "There's such power in simple beauty," she said as I eased the car onto the main road.

"I always sense the profound mystery of life in places like that," I responded.

"Does it make you want to go back to church?" she asked as she looked over at me and smiled.

"Would kissing a beautiful woman be part of the deal?"

"Not in the sanctuary, but if you got me in the sacristy with all that wine. Well, who knows what might happen!"

"I'd bless you first."

"You ministers have the most creative lines."

"I guess that's why they call us fathers."

"Oh, you're a cute one," she said as she turned toward me laughing. It wasn't long before she was fiddling with the radio looking for NPR. I was glad we had something in common with NPR. She was so quick and witty, and I felt a little pale in contrast, a lot like that bland rock that was sitting on the floor in the back seat of the car. Maybe opposites attract I thought as Abby located the station, leaned her seat back slightly, closed her eyes, and was soon asleep. I listened to Brahms, Vivaldi, and Mozart the rest of the way home, reflecting on the events of the day and all that was happening inside me.

I was feeling like a teenager. There was no getting around it. Over the last two days I had had some awkward moments and made some silly remarks while trying to impress. And then I had a comforting, intriguing thought. Maybe she's going through the same yips. Maybe it works both ways. The rock expedition was not normal behavior for a professional woman in her mid-forties.

Such were the thoughts that floated through me on that trip home from the churches. The sad thing was that it was all rapidly coming to an end. I looked over at her briefly as I turned the car onto route 421 for the final leg of the journey, and she was still sound asleep. She looked so beautiful and peaceful with her slow, steady, rhythmic breathing that somehow seemed to be in sync with the Brahms symphony that was quietly providing background music. As I turned the car into the Broyhill Center, I patted her thigh to wake her from her nap. "We're back," I said as I looked over at her. She rather dreamily looked up at me and smiled.

"Do we have to be? I'm not sure I want the afternoon to be over." She straightened the seat, stretched, and after a brief pause she continued. "I feel badly about having to go home tomorrow. Two more days would have been just great."

"We can get back together soon. My park work is about to lessen dramatically for the next five months."

"Would you come visit us in Durham? I would love for you to meet the twins."

"Just give me a date," I said as I grabbed her left hand and squeezed it. "Maybe we can plan it around a Duke football game. I would love to reconnect with Scott's coach."

"Sounds like a plan," she said as I eased the car into the parking lot. We both exited the car, and I moved around toward her. "I don't want to make a scene, Jeff. So just one brief kiss. I had a fantastic two days, and we may have something real between us. I look forward to working on it over the next few months."

"Me too," I said as I placed my arms round her and gave her more than a brief kiss. She responded with enthusiasm, and as we separated, I made her an offer that I had been thinking about for the last half hour. "Listen, before you go, let me make you and your friend a little offer. Woodlands is a fun restaurant in Blowing Rock, and they have this great guitar player if you like sixties music. I'm sure your friend knows where it is. If you are looking for a place to eat tonight, you might want to try it. The owner, Robert, is a friend of mine, and you can put the meal on my tab. I'm a regular at the place."

"Sounds good to me," she said as she broke our embrace and turned toward the inn. "I'll mention it to Judy, and thanks again for a perfectly splendid day. We'll be in touch," she concluded with that wonderful smile. I returned to the car with a big lump in my throat.

∗   ∗   ∗

They arrived at Woodlands about 7:30 p.m. I was in the middle of Bob Dylan's *Mister Tambourine Man*. The evening was no longer routine! I continued through the song as they were seated. It took Abby awhile to realize it was me on stage. I winked at her, her expression was one of shock, and then she giggled and poked her friend. They were both laughing as I started into a Neil Diamond tune.

"Welcome to Woodlands," I said into the mic after finishing the song. "Home of the best pork burrito in the High Country. What a day it was today. I hope you were all outside enjoying it. October won't last forever. I'd like to close this set with an old John Denver song, and then one you all know by James Taylor. The Taylor song is North Carolina's national anthem. The Denver tune was inspired by his ex-wife. Because nobody wants to dedicate a song to ex-wives, let's do this one for new girl-friends."

As I started *Annie's Song* with the familiar line that spoke so directly to my new feelings, "You fill up my senses, like a night in the forest," I looked over and winked at Abby. She smiled and gave me a big thumbs up. When I concluded the song a few minutes later, the polite applause that followed didn't matter. I was so intent on making Denver's simple message of love into my own that the audience faded from my awareness. I sang directly to Abby.

After finishing Taylor's *Carolina On My Mind*, I laid my guitar against the chair, stepped off the little stage, and walked toward Abby's table. On the way there, I ran into Heidi, one of my favorite waitresses. She was an ASU student who reminded me so much of Brenda. "Hey, Heidi. Would you bring me a draft of a light micro brew to the table with the two women on the left against the wall?"

"Sure thing, Mr. Peterson. *Annie's Song* sounded great. Got a new girlfriend?"

"I'll let you know next week," I said as I watched her move along to her table with several orders in her small hands. It always amazed me how waitresses like Heidi could carry so many dishes at one time. I stopped to shake the hand of a Park contributor from Valle Crucis, and then I was at Abby's table.

"Hi there, ladies. Have you ordered yet?" I asked, standing over them with a smile.

"Jeff, I don't believe this. I thought you had Park work tonight. This is quite a surprise. You're really good."

"Thanks, Abby, and you must be Judy," I said as I shifted my focus from Abby to her friend.

"Yes, it's very nice to meet you, Jeff. I've been here before when you were singing. When Abby said there was a good guitar player at Woodlands, I agreed with her."

"That was just part of the hype to get you here," I laughed. "And besides, you could have heard the person I share the job with. Her name is Beth Hagey. She's a thirty-year old music teacher in Boone."

"Nope. I'm pretty sure it was you. Can you join us for dinner?" Judy asked.

"Yeah. That's the least we can do since this one's on you," Abby chimed in with a smile.

"No. It's on Robert," I corrected her with a grin. "But I would love to join you. Heidi is bringing me a beer," I said as I pulled up a chair.

"Jeff, this is amazing. When did you start playing here?" Abby asked.

"About six months ago."

"That's about when I was here with my husband," Judy said.

"Well, I hope I didn't sound too nervous. This is certainly a new thing for me. Anyway, to get back to the job, it was good timing. They lost their other regular, and I needed the money. I make almost as much here as I do at the Park."

"I wish I had paid more attention the last time I was here," Judy said.

"Few people pay attention. I do it because I really love to sing. Most of what I sing resonates from some place deep inside me. It always frustrated me that as a minister I had no time to do this sort of thing." At that point Heidi came with my beer and took orders from Abby and Judy. Abby ordered a pork burrito, at least one person paid attention, and Judy ordered a barbecue chicken plate.

"Have you eaten, Jeff?" Abby asked.

"Yes, I had a barbecue sandwich and some fries about 5:45, just after I dropped you off. Did Abby tell you we went to see the Fresco churches today?"

"Yes, she did," Judy responded. "But she said that Luther's Rock was her favorite spot."

"Jefferson State Park is a fun place to have lunch," I said as I winked over at Abby. "Did she tell you about the damn rocks?" I asked as I directed my focus back to Judy.

"No, she didn't say anything about rocks."

"Ask her about them on the way home. They were the highlight of my day," I said with a smile as I glanced back at Abby. The conversation went on like this until their dinner arrived about fifteen minutes later. I stole a few fries from Abby's plate, finished my beer, and stood up to go. I walked around to Judy, took her hand in both of mine, and shook it warmly. "It's nice to meet you, Judy. Come back again with your husband. I'd like to meet him too."

"Will do Jeff, and thanks for dinner."

"Any time," I said while smiling down at her. And then I walked behind Abby and put both hands gently on her shoulders. "Got any requests, Abby?" I asked. She looked up at me and softly said:

"No, but thanks for *Annie's Song*." I squeezed her shoulders gently.

"Promise me you won't leave without coming up to say goodbye."

"We'll come see you with the check."

Chapter 8

Beaver Dam

TWO MONTHS LATER WE were back together at Woodlands. This time it was Abby's surprise. I was performing my usual Thursday night gig, and she arrived a little before eight. I hurried to finish the set so I could join her at her table.

"Is the tab still on you?" she asked as she got up from the table. "I'm hungry. It was a long drive." I threw my arms around her and hugged her tight.

"Wow—what a surprise!" I said as I sat down on the chair across from her.

"It was my turn," she said as she smiled across at me.

"How about another pork burrito? I could use a beer."

"That worked really well last time."

"Good. Let me go find a waitress." Susan Perlman was covering our area. I finally found her in the kitchen. Upon returning, I said: "Susan promised to rush the order."

"You can have most of my fries."

"Where are you staying? You know we may be getting snow tonight. I was thinking of leaving a little early."

"The forecast I heard on the way up was for a mix of snow and rain. It's supposed to last most of tomorrow."

"That's mountain weather."

"With regard to your question, I was hoping to stay at Beaver Dam, but I haven't made reservations yet."

"You've got one. You're the best," and I reached across the table to grab both of her hands. "I'm free all weekend except that I'm back here on Saturday night."

"I can branch out and have a chicken dinner then."

"I can't believe this," I said as Susan came with our order.

"As I just said, it was my turn. Even the twins enjoyed your visit three weeks ago."

"That's good. Sometimes those initial visits can be difficult for kids."

"They loved mingling with the Duke players after the game. They couldn't believe you were a friend of the coach."

"I wouldn't say we were friends," I said after sipping my beer. "But I certainly have a lot of respect for him. Scott viewed him as a second father even though he was only with him for a year."

"You might be surprised to learn about a call I received at the office last week. Coach Kelly wants to get together for dinner the next time you're in town."

"That is a nice surprise. Now listen, Abby. As you may have noticed, we have a thin crowd. I'm sure it's the weather problem. Finish up your dinner, and we'll leave in half an hour. No later than 8:45. I'm going to end with Annie's Song," and I smiled across at her while grabbing my beer to return to work.

"Just no dedication please," she said returning my smile.

＊　＊　＊

"Jesus Jeff," she said after shutting the door following our rather long, tandem drive to my home in Bethel. "Thank you for taking it easy on your monstrous mountain roads. That's the scariest trip I have ever taken."

"You did great. Now hurry up that hill. That light you see up there marks the only door to my place. Do you have a suitcase in the trunk?'

"Just one and a small duffel."

"The weather sucks, so don't wait for me. I'll grab your stuff, and meet you in the house. The door's unlocked." I met her in the living room, and she was taking it all in. She enthused over the rustic look, and wondered if the Vermont casting wood stove was my only source of heat.

"It's a little cold in here, don't you think?"

"I'll crank up the stove, and you can nose around. As soon as I get the fire going, I'll give you a tour."

"No rush. I'll check out your library." While the house gained warmth, I took her to Brenda's room, and then she climbed the ladder to the third-floor cupola by herself.

"The view will be a whole lot better tomorrow," I said looking up at her.

"It's snowing out there. We may be stranded here for a few days."

"I have food and plenty of wood."

"I just hope we get a little sun while I'm here," she said as she descended the ladder. "I don't want to miss the beautiful setting you've talked so much about."

"Maybe by tomorrow afternoon," I said as I followed her down the stairs from Brenda's room. When we arrived in the living room, she took my hand and led me through the kitchen into what was soon to become our bedroom. Upon arrival, she looked up at me with a sheepish grin and said:

"I think this room is finally warm enough." I took her in my arms and kissed her passionately. She broke away before I was ready with a look of determination. "Jeff, I'm not usually this forward, but you have been so patient. You made two trips to Durham, and I guess you noticed our little house was pretty crowded. The twins always seemed to be around. Anyway, I have really appreciated your patience and lack of complaints. You have been a great sport," and she gently kissed me.

"It's a topic I'm not so good at talking about."

"Well, there's no need for any more talking because we're about to get deadly serious. The last person to get their clothes off and under those sheets does the dishes tomorrow morning." And she ran to the far side of the bed and was under the sheets before I had unbuttoned my shirt. It was a beautiful performance, and a contest I was happy to finish in second place.

As I started walking toward the bed, Abby peeked up from under the covers and smiled sheepishly up at me. "Is this safe?" she asked softly.

I stopped and looked down at her. "This is the first time for me in more than four years. My only other partner was my ex."

"Good," she said with those playful blue eyes dancing. "Looks like I'm getting something close to a virgin. One more little note of caution. I'm prone to having twins, you know."

"Don't worry about that," I said while looking down at her. "I had a vasectomy right after Scott was born."

"Are you interested in my history?" she asked in a tone of voice that was gentle and reassuring.

"Not really. It's been too long for me to care much about that."

"Can you make up for the two visits we lost dodging the twins?" she whispered as I climbed into her arms. I held her tightly and could find no immediate words of reply. I was beyond excitement, and yet I also felt a little awkward as the teenage image bubbled up from inside me.

I moved slightly away from her and looked at her face. She opened her eyes, and they sparkled. I looked down at her breasts. They were so beautiful. Slowly I refocused my gaze to her face and softly said, "I feel more like we've lost thirty years." She pulled me toward her, and her hands moved up and down my body. This was not about teasing, contests, or silly games. It was about her real desire to express passion and care. My hands responded in a reciprocating manner, and deep inside her I became whole again, a man who was finally able to love a woman with a deep commitment and with all of his heart. Powerful emotions flooded through me, and a loneliness which had placed a scar on my heart passed into history.

*　*　*

I was up well before Abby. It was still dark outside and raining hard. I stoked the fire, took a quick shower, and shaved. I was thumbing through "The Economist" which defines my political world, when I heard the shower again. She soon joined me in the living room, and I jumped up to kiss her good morning.

"Hungry?" I finally asked as I broke away from her.

"Always," she responded with a warm smile.

"I have raisin bran and toast, or we can do scrambled eggs and bacon."

"Let's keep the dishes you're doing to a minimum. Raisin bran will be fine."

"Can we have another contest for the dinner dishes?"

"For some reason, you're not as tongue tied over this issue as you claimed to be last night."

"It's called psychological growth."

"I would choose other words to explain it; but if you behave yourself, we'll see," she responded wagging her finger at me and laughing. As I walked into the kitchen, she went to look out a window. "Yuk," she said. "Do you have a good rainy-day program?"

"You know what I was thinking. I would love to write a song together. Your poetry is terrific. Have you ever tried writing a lyric?"

"No, but I think I could manage that?"

"Great! Let's do it. I already have a title. I would have been singing in the shower, but I wanted to let you sleep."

"What's the title?" she said as she walked from the living room to join me in the kitchen. "Just one piece of toast. Raisin toast will be a treat."

"I was thinking something like "Peace Begins With Me.""

"I thought you didn't want to read *War and Peace*."

"You're right. The title does sound like it comes from Tolstoy."

"I like the title," she said as she sat down at the kitchen table, "but my cooperation is conditional."

"What's the catch?"

"That I read your resignation letter first. I bet you thought I was going to forget about it."

"I guess I was hoping you would, but you have a deal." It took us to after lunch to get to the song.

"What do you mean about the salvation story being a massive consumer fraud?" Abby asked after we had settled in the living room with a second cup of coffee. "That's quite an indictment."

"This may turn into a long theological discussion," I replied as I looked across at her on the couch. *

"It's raining, Jeff, and I'm a PhD. I thrive on these discussions every now and then. The floor is yours."

"Okay. I've got plenty more coffee. Now where to begin. I guess the best place is with a little Jewish religious history. Salvation is a Jewish idea. A long way back, God made a covenant with Israel in which she promised to protect Israel in return for Jews obeying God's law."

"I never thought of God making covenants; but if God's a girl, I guess anything is possible."

"Moses certainly thought God made covenants. With regard to this one, it worked pretty well for a long time. Israel thrived under Kings David and Solomon."

"What time frame are we talking about?"

"Around 1,000 BC. Things started falling apart after Solomon's death. Israel split into a northern and southern kingdom. This weakened state allowed Assyria to conquer the Northern Kingdom in the 8th century BC, and Babylonia captured Judah, the Southern Kingdom, 200 years later. As a result, Israel became a colonized nation.

"How could this happen? The covenant said that God was supposed to protect Israel."

"You can drop the female pronoun," Abby said with a laugh. "It sounds like God has become a loser."

"Actually, the prophets had an answer to that question. God was no longer protecting Israel because Israel had sinned. Israel was responsible for breaking the covenant, not God."[1]

"That's exactly what fundamentalists always say. God is never wrong. Such and such a disaster occurred because it was in some way part of God's plan."

"Really nice, Abby. I couldn't agree more. The prophetic message was not only punishment, however. Their collective anger about Israel's sin was always tempered by words of hope. That hope was salvation. The idea was that God was just, and that he would honor his covenant by sending a messiah to rescue Israel. The messiah in the person of a king or a great military leader would restore Israel's glory as a nation. This messiah would establish God's kingdom on earth.

"Jesus accepted this idea of salvation. The central focus of his message was that this coming kingdom of God was imminent, that it would come within the generation of his followers. In fact, God was already battling the forces of evil to achieve this result during Jesus's lifetime."

"Did Jesus make his message a prediction?"

"Yes. He tells his followers time and time again that God's kingdom was coming within their lifetimes. He urged them to get ready for its coming by turning their lives around and honoring God."

"Then Jesus was wrong. This kingdom you say he talked about never came into history. This is amazing. The Son of God making such a mistake."

"You're good, Abby. If the truth be known, Jesus was a failed prophet."

"I know I'm good, Jeffie. I proved that last night. But to get back to your lecture, this is really quite unbelievable, which leads me to ask one more question. If Jesus was a failed prophet, how come there are two billion Christian believers today?"

"That's a really good question. First century Palestine had several of these failed prophets who preached the imminent coming of God's messiah. That idea was "in the air." If they became popular with large followings, like

---

1. For readers interested in the biblical passages that support Jeff's argument on the salvation myth, please see the Appendix.

with Jesus, Rome had them executed. Once dead, you never heard about them again.

"But Jesus was different. To explain the success of Christianity, we need to briefly return to Jewish salvation history. I told you the answer the prophets gave to explain Israel's colonization, that the people of Israel had sinned, that they were not keeping God's laws. That answer worked for many years until the second century BC. At that time, a nasty Syrian king came into power who wanted to increase his country's control over Israel."

"So now the Syrians controlled Israel?"

"Yes, and I can't remember the exact dates, but this king, Antiochus Epiphanes the IVth, tried to destroy the Jewish religion. He ordered icons of Greek gods to be installed in the Temple at Jerusalem, and he began executing Jews for circumcising their children. Jews were now being punished for obeying God's law. The answer from the prophets no longer worked.

"Into this void of meaning and despair, the prophet Daniel came to the rescue. Daniel argued that Israel's misery was not the result of divine punishment, but rather the actions of Satan, the power of evil. This Satan was out to control the world. God, however, would honor his promises. There would soon come an "end times," a time that was so bad God would intervene to rescue the righteous among the people of Israel. He would do that by sending his divine agent, the Son of Man, from the clouds of heaven to judge the people of Israel and rescue the righteous by taking them to heaven.

"So now we have two different concepts of salvation. When Jesus died, his followers were devastated. Jesus was both charismatic and a great lover. His followers truly worshipped him. Not long after the crucifixion, these followers began having visions of Jesus alive in heaven. The Book of Acts talks about these vision experiences. Paul had one, Stephen had one, several apostles had one. It wasn't long before these followers of Jesus were convinced he was alive in heaven."

"Is this what the resurrection is all about?"

"Yes and no. Not a physical resurrection. The four stories in the gospels about a physical resurrection are a mess. There are so many differences between them that all credibility for this central Christian belief disappears. The gospel writers cannot even agree as to where the resurrection took place. Matthew puts it on a mountain in Galilee while Luke has it at someone's home in Jerusalem. These glaring differences cannot be reconciled. Here we have the most amazing event ever alleged to have taken place in human history, and the gospel writers disagree as to where it happened. Unbelievable!"

"You're gently blowing my mind. I wish I was taping this. There's a lot to remember. It's a good thing I'm drinking coffee and not wine."

"Some rainy day in the future when we're together we can do a comparison study of the gospel resurrection stories; but for now, getting back to the main point of our discussion, Paul in 1 Corinthians claims that his vision experience was the same resurrection encounter the disciples had following the crucifixion. Resurrection for the disciples was a vision experience, not the physical event described in the gospels. The only difference was that Paul was the last person to receive one. For Paul, there was no physical resurrection. He comments several times that flesh and blood do not inherit the kingdom of God. And we so often forget. Paul was the first one to write about the resurrection of Jesus.

"Okay, the time has come for me to wrap this up. We now have with Daniel another concept of God's messiah. He's not a political leader or a general, but a cosmic judge who has resided with God from the beginning of time. Salvation will now take place in heaven, and no longer apply to the land of Israel. Upon reflection, Paul and many others of Jesus's followers began to think of Jesus's death in light of Daniel. Jesus was the messiah who had to suffer on the cross, but God rewarded him for his obedience by taking him to heaven. He was now sitting at God's right hand and would soon return from the clouds of heaven to rescue the righteous among Jesus's followers and take them to heaven. This return of Jesus as the Son of Man as prophesized by Daniel was also seen as imminent."

"Two quick comments to make sure I'm understanding you. First, salvation no longer pertains to Israel as a corporate group, but rather to individual followers of Jesus."

"Yes."

"And second. Paul and many among Jesus's followers also made a prediction of Jesus's imminent return as the Son of Man that never materialized in history?"

"Yes, and the process of reflection continued. Over time Jesus was made into a supernatural being. The gospel of John began to think of Jesus as God's divine son, an idea that Church councils in the fourth and fifth centuries proclaimed as a central part of church doctrine. Belief in Jesus Christ as your savior would guarantee you a place in heaven. Jesus had not only become divine, but an equal to God as the second arm of the trinity.

The answer to your question of why Christianity took off and flourished now becomes easy to answer. Salvation in heaven was an attractive idea to sell. Everyone wants to beat death."

"Jesus never preached such a salvation, did he?"

"No. The idea originated with Daniel and was embellished by the early church. As I have been saying, we have two very different concepts of salvation—that of Jesus and that of Paul and the early church."

"Was Jesus ever alive in heaven?"

"That's a question I cannot answer, but he never became the Son of Man predicted in Daniel's prophecy. But to get back to the question, it could have been a psychological event in the minds of his closest followers. There is plenty of evidence such a thing can happen when you lose someone you deeply loved."

"I see what you mean by consumer fraud. The whole idea of salvation is based on predictions that never materialized and premises that have no relevance for the 20th century."

"Right. The salvation idea applies to specific assumptions made in ancient Israel which never worked out and have no relevance to our lives."

"And so that is why you left the church?"

"In part it explains it, but there were some personal issues I was dealing with that made the situation so much worse. You know about my failed marriage and the death of Scott. In addition, I was trying to sort out some nasty experiences I had in Vietnam."

"Interesting."

"If you don't mind, I would like to leave the Vietnam stuff for another time. Maybe when the sun is shining."

"Does the sun ever shine in these mountains?"

"It certainly did while you were here in October."

"You got me on that. I will be happy to do the dishes after lunch, and I will give you a pass on Vietnam for now because I have a question more relevant to what we have been discussing."

"That's nice," I said smiling over at her.

"Here's my question. If salvation is a myth, why be a Christian? Is there any point to it?"

"Thanks for the question. It allows me to finish on a positive note. I see two good reasons for remaining a Christian. The first is the teachings of Jesus. They guide my life. We live in a society in which racial injustice remains a problem. There are large gaps in wealth between the top and the bottom tiers of the economy, and Presidents have a habit of sending troops to fight stupid wars. If Christians would only take the teachings of Jesus seriously, we could make progress in solving these problems.

"The second relates to certain features in modern life. There's a huge need for the Christian religion, maybe more now than ever. We live in a highly competitive, isolating society. As work has become more mechanized, it has lost its meaning. Urban cities do not have the emotional warmth of small towns in more rural areas. How do people cope with isolation and a loss of meaning? Left on their own, so many of them commit suicide or turn to drugs.

"Christian communities are one of the best solutions to this problem of alienation. Jesus created loving communities to deal with the problem of Rome. Roman colonial rule was oppressive. The problem was that if you fought Rome it would lead to mass slaughter and economic devastation. By creating loving communities, Jesus helped to empower people which enabled them to ignore Roman colonial oppression.

"The Book of Acts talks about these communities. Establishing them was a central part of Jesus's mission. We can certainly learn from his example. When people are loved and cared for within a community, their hearts expand. It changes the way they see the world. It provides for a sense of joy and meaning in life. A loving community is the best antidote I know to alienation and fear.

"Let me tell you a personal story, and then we will end this little sermon."

"I don't see you as preaching at all. You are providing interesting answers to my questions. I got you into this."

"I'm glad you see it that way, but to get back to my story. When Scott was killed in Charleston, our church came to the rescue. At first I was in shock after hearing the news, and then Rebecca and I went emotionally dead. As the news got out and news like that always does, people came to our parish home. They brought food, and their loving presence. We celebrated Scott's life. Many of his high school friends were there. We cried and laughed, and they held us in their arms. Love was floating all over that parish hall. It was a profound experience, really the most profound religious experience of my life. People kept on caring several months later. Rebecca accepted their care, and recovered nicely. Like a jerk, I ignored it, put on a mask that all was well, and ran from the church six months later."

Abby left the couch and walked over to me. I got up with her, and we embraced. "You're so honest with yourself, Jeff. That's just one of the reasons I have fallen in love with you. It was a good lecture. You answered all of my questions, and now the rest of the day is yours."

*　*　*

We made love after the lecture. It was less awkward, less urgent, but deeply satisfying. Abby made lunch by adding chicken to a salad I had saved from the other day. I was nervous the salad had become a little wimpy, but her touch was able to give it new life. I helped her with the few dishes, and then the fun work began. I got my guitar, a yellow pad, and pen for her.

"'Peace Begins With Me.' I like the title. Let's start by throwing out images that speak to it, and I'll write them down," Abby said as she took a seat on the couch.

"Bridges, a place of refuge, engaging with those who are different."

"Nice Jeff. What about the individual? A smile, a laugh, a song to sing."

"Tranquility, still waters, the brotherhood of man."

"Slow down, Bud. I'm having trouble getting them all down."

"You need a break for some tea," I said as I left my rocking chair and headed for the kitchen. "I was thinking of tea leaves, and it just sounded good. I've got all flavors."

"Plain is good for me."

"How about herbal? I might go with strawberry."

"Herbal would be great."

"Swords into Plowshares," I called out from the kitchen.

"This is fascinating, Jeff. Your images are societal. Mine are of individuals."

"It starts in here, Abby," and I pounded my chest. "From there it moves out in wider circles."

"Nice. Okay. Let's do this in three verses. The first will relate to inner peace, the second with societal peace, and we'll end with world peace."

"Perfect," I said as I placed her tea on the table. "You work on a lyric, and I'll experiment with my guitar." We were quiet for half an hour, maybe a little longer, before I broke the silence with: "How does this sound?" I played a series of chords introducing the song, and then I went to a melody line that was admittedly incomplete.

"I like the tune and mood of what you have there, but how do we fit it to the words of my lyric?"

"What do you have written?"

"A draft of two verses."

"Great!" And I left my chair to join her on the couch. Let me see it." She handed me the yellow pad, and I read through what she had written. "The first verse is terrific. I like what the first two lines of the second verse say, but they seem a little wooden. Maybe wordy is a better way to put it."

"I agree. They are too wordy. I'll continue working on them." I left the room to get myself a second yellow pad and pen. When I returned, I copied down the first verse. "I'll try to put these words to music," I said as I kissed her cheek before returning to my seat on the opposite end of my small living room. Again, we were quiet, focused on the task at hand, when Abby broke the silence after listening to me messing around with my guitar.

"Jeff, the melody line is a little harsh, strident. Try toning it down some. Our song is about peace." Without looking up, I closed my eyes, and tried softening the tone. Before long I was able to say:

"How's this?" Abby listened intently and responded.

"Much better. I have fixed the second verse, and I'm almost finished with the last one."

Good. Can I read your writing?"

"I have a lot of cross outs."

"Can you rewrite it on a clean sheet of paper, and then we can try to sing it together. In the meantime, I need to hit the head." Upon returning, I picked up my guitar and joined her on the couch. Actually, I more than joined her. I about sat on her lap, showering her with kisses.

"Jeff, for God's sake. Let me finish this."

"I was just trying to add a little inspiration."

"Well, with that sweaty face all I got was a lot of perspiration which I don't need." Five minutes later, maybe a little less, she looked up from the notepad and smiled. "There," and she handed the pad to me. "Now you can kiss me and tell me what a good lyricist I am."

I did both. We continued to work on our new song, fitting the music to the words for another half an hour or so, and then I talked Abby into learning an old Johnny Cash song, "If I Were A Carpenter." I had a devilish plan for Woodlands on Saturday night which I kept to myself. It came to me in a flash of intuition after hearing her sing. She has a beautiful voice.

Abby rapidly lost interest, however. After the third take of the song, she got up from the couch and walked over to the window. "Jeff, it's five o'clock and still raining. I think we need a new venue. How about we go out for dinner? The snow has gone from the roads with all this rain. Getting out would be a nice change."

"I love Chinese."

"Can you cook it?"

"Way above my skill level."

"Then let's go out. I love Chinese too. It's my treat."

"I thought guys were supposed to pick up such tabs."

"They are, but you sometimes wonder about guys who live in one-bedroom shacks."

"Two bedrooms. You forgot about upstairs."

"I stand corrected. You can pay."

"I know just the place." Three hours later we fought about the check with Abby finally winning. It was a great end to a fun day.

*   *   *

There is one additional event that needs reporting from that wonderful surprise weekend. We went to see "Apollo 13" on Saturday afternoon, took a long, spirited walk around the town of Blowing Rock, the weather had improved but it was cold, and then it was off to Woodlands.

It was a rather routine night. We had dinner there early, and then Abby sipped wine and talked on and off with Robert while waiting for me to do my thing. My thing changed dramatically, however, toward the end of the last set.

After acknowledging the polite applause for "San Francisco Bay Blues," one of my favorites, I announced: "Folks you are about to hear a Woodlands first. I wrote my first song this afternoon called "Peace Begins With Me," and it just so happens that my lyricist is here in the audience. I can't do this song without her being up here with me. So please welcome to the stage Ms. Abby Dunbar."

Abby was dumbstruck, and remained seated at her table in the far corner. "Folks, she's going to need some encouragement," and I began calling out. "Abby, Abby." Soon the audience joined the chorus. Abby eventually surrendered to the good-natured pressure, and joined me on the stage.

"I hate you," she whispered before turning to face the audience.

"I hope that will pass," I whispered back as I began the intro to the song. We sang the first verse with good harmony, and she was even able to return my smile as I looked across at her.

> Let peace begin with me, I say
> Let me smile, laugh, and sing today.
> Throw out anger, envy, and fear
> Let the sun shine throughout the year.
> Let the sun shine throughout the year.

After finishing the first verse, a guitar solo followed. Abby looked out at the audience while jabbing a finger at me and spoke into the mic: "Guitar solo folks. I haven't yet written the chorus." Considerable laughter rang out. The second verse also went well.

> Let me treat those around me with love and care
> Let me create a place of refuge for those here and there.
> Engaging people who are different defines what is right
> Building bridges not walls is my delight.
> Building bridges not walls is my delight.

As we did the third verse. Abby's voice gained in depth and confidence.

> A peaceful me creates a world at rest
> Turning swords into plowshares works the best.
> Money can't buy it, sad but true
> And so I say it's up to you.
> It's up to you.

When the song ended, Abby smiled at the audience and started to exit the stage. The applause was enthusiastic, and I quickly raised my hand to quiet it. "Call her back folks. I'm not finished with her yet."

The audience dutifully responded with "Abby, Abby," and she slowly returned.

"You're going to pay for this," she whispered as she returned to the stage.

"I owe you for last night's dinner," I whispered back and then turned slightly to face the audience. "While we're on the topic of war songs, I want to do my all-time favorite, Dylan's "Blowing in the Wind." In some ways this song will never do justice to Abby's wonderful voice, but we do sing it well together. I want to dedicate the song to war veterans from around the world. I am a war veteran myself, and all I can tell you is that Dylan is right. War is a mean, nasty business."

The song went extremely well, and again the applause was enthusiastic. As Abby started to exit the stage a second time, I grabbed her elbow and wouldn't let her go. She got the message and remained with me. I then announced to the audience, "For our last song of the night, I want to do 'If I Were a Carpenter.' You old Johnny Cash fans will remember that the song became famous when Johnny sang it with his wife June Carter Cash. Early on in the song, June Carter sings 'I'd marry you anyway. I'd have your baby.' I don't think that's in the cards for me after these last ten minutes."

"You've got that right," Abby forthrightly spoke into the mic. The Woodlands crowd went wild. When the laughter quieted down, I began the song. Abby sang her part with gusto, and the applause was again enthusiastic. I took her hand, and we left the stage together. When the applause continued and even deepened, I dropped her hand and returned to the stage.

"Thank you. Thank you for that wonderful support. I think you touched my beautiful lyricist too. Please, everybody stand. Let's sing together North Carolina's state anthem, James Taylor's 'Carolina on my Mind.'"

I returned to our table at the back of the room after ending the song, and Abby was talking with a woman from the table next to us. Soon Robert came on the scene. "You were fantastic Abby," Robert enthused while breaking into Abby's conversation with her first fan. "We need you here as a regular."

"Are you crazy!"

"You're good, girl. I mean really good."

"Thanks Robert. I hate to admit it, but I come with a good lead singer."

"When are you coming back?"

"That's up to him," and she pointed to me smiling.

"I hope it's soon," Robert said smiling across at Abby.

"Me too," I said quietly as I placed my guitar in its case.

Chapter 9

A Tantric Blessing

ABBY RETURNED TO THE mountains on Monday May 12th, arriving a little before noon. She was here to celebrate the end of her semester at Chapel Hill. The twins would be with their father until Friday.

We had been together twice during the winter—once around New Years and then during President's week in February. We had great fun skiing at Beech and Sugar. It was especially good for me because I was able to improve my relationship with the twins under fun circumstances.

Abby even performed one set with me at Woodlands. The twins were really impressed with their mother. I was thrilled because she seemed to really enjoy it which boded well for a new venture I was going to spring on her at some point during the week.

My plan for the visit was to spend one night at Delphi. Tuesday and Thursday nights were out because of Woodlands, and the forecast for Wednesday was not good. As a result, I fed her a quick lunch, and we were on the trail by 1 p.m. I carried our dinner in my pack along with a sleeping bag, blanket, water, the utensils we would need, and a bottle of red wine. Abby carried a second sleeping bag, a blanket, more water, and a bottle of white wine. I hoped I hadn't forgotten something.

The sun was bright, a mild 62, with little wind. The mountains projected a soft blue haze, a quality for which they are famous, which diminished with distance. Abby enthused over the scenery and was especially pleased with the trail because we could walk side by side which made conversation easy.

"Where are we headed?" she asked as we walked down the hill from the house.

"I thought we'd go first to a lovely meadow about an hour from here. It has this enormous flat rock that makes it unique. Eventually we're going to Delphi, as I explained on the phone."

"Why the name? I remember you talking about this place, but I don't remember why you named it Delphi."

"It's an eerie, beautiful place. Rebecca and I went to Delphi in Greece thirty years ago when we were in Europe. You can certainly understand why people believed the gods communicated with them there."

"I see. This Delphi place is where you're taking me for dinner and the night, an eerie place in the wilderness where some New Age gods are going to communicate with us. Some girls get all the luck!"

"You may have second thoughts about me."

"I don't think so," she said as she smiled over at me.

"That's nice, but can we change the conversation."

"Sure, what's up?"

"I'd love to know a little more of your history."

"You weren't too interested when all my clothes were off if I remember correctly." I smiled thinking how great she looked then.

"Badly phrased. I'd love to know a little more about Gar. You often speak so fondly of him."

"Do I detect a little jealousy?" She said as she grabbed onto my left hand.

"I wouldn't say jealousy. You just seem to do really well with him after the divorce."

"Did you ever go to Club 47 in Cambridge?"

"All the time. They had the best folk artists in the country performing there."

"I met my husband at a Joan Baez performance."

"What was he doing in Cambridge?"

"He was getting his PhD in applied mathematics. I fall for the tall, dark, and handsome ones," she said as she squeezed my hand, leaned up, and gently kissed me. Her blue eyes were shining.

"Is he Hindu?"

"Yes, a practicing one of sorts, though it was hard to do in Durham. He comes from a prominent Indian family in Delhi. His Dad is a top diplomat in the Foreign Ministry."

"How did you get along with his family?"

"Not well. They refused to come to the wedding. I thought things would get better when the twins came along, but it didn't seem to change things much."

"What happened to the marriage?"

"There were value differences. He wanted a more Indian family, and I am an American woman with a PhD with some interest in a career."

"I bet his parents were part of the problem."

"Huge. The crisis came in 1988. I was busy with two little girls and teaching. He was consumed with work. Our sex life had become routine and far less frequent. During all this, his mother was diagnosed with pancreatic cancer."

"She was given a death sentence."

"Yes, and he was very close to her. Upon hearing the news, he immediately returned to India for what turned out to be almost four months. I was making plans to take the twins there after the semester in May. The first hint of a problem came when he told us not to come. At the time, it never occurred to me he was having an affair. His family was probably busy arranging a marriage. Anyway, to shorten the story, he returned at the end of June practically engaged. A year later we were divorced."

"I bet it was tough."

"It was because I really loved him, despite our cultural differences. But as you know we have managed to become friends again, and he has been a great provider."

"What does he do?"

"That's an interesting question. I finished my dissertation in the spring of 1980, and we were married that June. He still had two more years at MIT. Harvard helped us considerably by giving me two, one-year appointments. I received the tenure track position at Chapel Hill in 1982.

"When Gar finished his PhD in the spring of '82, high tech companies from all over the place made offers—IBM, Wang Labs, Microsoft, and there were others. My ex is really a software genius, but here's what makes his story interesting.

"That first year of our marriage he decided to put our cars under the same insurance policy. He made an appointment with a guy at Prudential, and it took fifty minutes to get a quote and fill out the paper work. It was all done by hand. On the subway back to our apartment, he knew exactly what he was going to do once his degree was in hand, and that was to create software for auto insurance companies.

"My job at Chapel Hill worked perfectly into his plans. We got a two-bedroom apartment, and he used one for an office. He spent two or three months studying the auto insurance business, and for some reason decided on State Farm. He then spent the next eighteen months designing this elegant, simple to use software to computerize the entire pricing process. It was a huge job because each state is different, and his programs had to be perfect. Every bug discovered. He signs his name to his work.

"I'll never forget the day he was finally finished. When I got back from school, he said we're going out to dinner, and then we're coming home to make babies. We're going to be rich.

"And he was right. He went to State Farm, to their office in Charlotte I think; and, of course, they loved his programs. They offered him a million dollars on the spot. Not nearly enough, he said. 'I'm going to Allstate,' and he got up and left."

"Did he go there?"

"It wasn't necessary. A week later some big shot at State Farm offered him ten million—five for the auto programs and five to create programs for their other products. They were terrified about what would happen if he went to a competitor."

"Wow—he's a smart cookie. Did all that money complicate the divorce?"

"No. It was amazing. I wondered how we would work it all out. Six months after we separated he called inviting me to lunch. He wanted to discuss the divorce in a public place to keep things civil and under control. At first I said no, but when he called a week later I relented. It was all to make things easier for the girls, he said.

"The meeting was pretty awkward at first; but when we got down to the real issues of the divorce, things went well. He began by thanking me for supporting him for four years. Half of the money is yours, he said. He also said that Sahi, his Indian honey, would hate our little house. So he paid off the mortgage, gave me the house, and half of the State Farm money. He had invested all of it. He refused to spend principal. It was his dream for us to retire early. Anyway, a week after that lunch, I opened an account at Dean Witter, and he had half of the shares from each company transferred to me."

"He does sound like a pretty good guy."

"The twins adore him as you know, though they're not too wild about Sahi. She's done very little to learn English. Our daughter Tara thinks they will soon be returning to India."

"Will he work for a software company over there?"

"I don't think so. He's had another big success. Just before he went back to India to say goodbye to his mother, he had started to study the health care industry. He recently sold an accounting package to a huge hospital chain. Now all he talks about is electronic records."

"What's that?"

"The idea is to computerize all patient records so they can be sent around the health care system electronically. He was explaining it to me about a month ago when he brought the girls home from a swim meet.

"It's a way to save huge amounts of money. Let's say you live in a small town with a community hospital. You have a problem, and have several tests done. They then send you to MGH or Duke. Typically the teaching hospital will repeat all the tests because the results are not right there before them. He hopes to send all records electronically."

"That does sound like a good idea."

"That's why he won't be going to India anytime soon except to visit, which is good for me. I think he will at least wait until the girls are out of high school before going back to India."

"Does he have kids with Sahi?"

"They have a two-year old little boy named Jaabin who is adorable. Note, however, the very Indian name. As I told you that first day, we chose names that reflected both cultures. Sahi is also expecting another in the next three or four months."

"I now see why you only work part-time."

"I don't really need to work, but I enjoy teaching. My life was going so well until you messed it up completely."

"Sorry about that. I know I snore. Are there other problems?"

"Well, to begin with, you don't like getting your feet wet in cold rivers. Should I continue?"

"I think I've heard enough."

"How much longer to that large rock you're taking me to?"

"Not far. No more than ten minutes."

"Just enough time. I did want to tell you about our recent book club meeting. You met most of the women at that party I gave after Thanksgiving. We discussed Wallace Stegner's *Angle of Repose*. He won the Pulitzer Prize for it in the 70's. Do you know it?"

"No, but I do remember reading *The Big Rock Candy Mountain* in high school."

"That's a good one too. *Angle of Repose* is a superbly written novel. It's the story of a married couple who are so completely different. She's an artist and writer, and he's an engineer—your stereotypical man from Mars, woman from Venus, though I really can't stand that analogy. It takes place in the late 1800s in the West. That causes another problem 'cuz Susan, the wife, is a committed Easterner and never really adjusts to her life in the West, which stresses their marriage. Despite these problems, their marriage is quite tender and loving in its own intriguing way.

"Our group focused mainly on Susan—that's why it might have been good if you had been there. Just this one time! Normally no men are allowed. Anyway, Susan was an interesting woman. A highly talented artist and writer who due to her husband's perpetual bad luck was often placed in the position of being the main breadwinner. And yet her career was clearly secondary to her husband's. She made all the compromises.

"You would have been interested in the powerful treatment of forgiveness that comes at the end of the book. Their marriage undergoes a crisis when she has an affair with a younger man, a man who considered Oliver, Susan's husband, as his mentor. We never know exactly what happens, they probably never had intercourse together, but they were off in the woods somewhere when the youngest daughter of Susan and Oliver drowns in a river. The tragedy is made so much worse because Susan and Oliver never talk about it, and he never forgives her. The result is their marriage is changed, there is a tension and a distance between them that plagues the last twenty-five years of their life together.

"As a matter of fact, the book is a must read for you. Oliver, the kindest, most decent of men, ruins his life because he keeps it all in."

"You're going to pester me about this, aren't you?"

"Maybe in a teasing way, but I'm not a nag. Some men just need a little coaching to help them express their emotions. I know you will tell me more about Scott and Vietnam when you're ready."

"It's a part of myself I really don't understand. In many ways I'm an open person, but there are places inside me I'm just shy about I guess."

"It's fine to keep parts to yourself as long as those parts are healthy and not hurting you or those around you who love and depend on you. But I'm not the preacher in this duo."

"Me neither. I'm not sure about much anymore except that you're a very special lady," and she squeezed my hand and looked over at me with blue eyes that glowed with warmth. We were quiet for a while, and I calculated that we would arrive at the large rock momentarily.

*   *   *

We stayed at that beautiful meadow for more than two hours with the warm May sun and the craggy face of Grandfather Mountain staring down at us. We were all alone at a very special place on a very special planet.

"Thirsty, Abby?" I asked as I lifted her pack from her shoulders and placed it on the large flat rock. The rock was large enough to hold thirty or forty people with its rounded edges touching the ground and its highest point not more than three feet off of the ground.

"Sure. What you got?"

"I brought a couple of bottles of wine and some diet and regular Cokes."

"Too early for the wine—way too early. The diet Coke sounds good." I lowered my pack and laid it on the rock and reached in for a diet and a regular Coke. "It even feels chilled. How did you manage that?" she asked as she accepted the can.

"I put them in the freezer for half an hour before we left."

"Tastes great. Now I need some expert advice as to where one pees around here. It's so open."

"Just go off about twenty-five yards and go. There's no one around for miles." I went off in the opposite direction. Upon returning, I took out the sleeping bag, folded it a few times to make a backrest, and placed it up against the rock. I was sitting there sipping my Coke when she returned.

"That wasn't so bad," she said as she sat down beside me.

"Good," I responded as I put my arm around her and pulled her close. "How did your exams go?"

"Pretty typical. About half were As. Honors students are generally highly motivated. I did hand back two Ds. The best thing is they're over."

"It's amazing you had two Ds."

"Some kids are just not emotionally ready for college. They need to spend some time working or in the military."

"And all their hormones are raging at eighteen."

"That doesn't seem to change much with age," she said as she nestled her head up against me.

"Thank goodness for that," I said as I pulled her closer. "And now you're free for almost four months. I'm looking forward to having the twins up here too."

"You're going to love this. I'm looking into a tennis camp for them up here. It is offered for all of July, and it will occupy them for most of the day. That will give me plenty of time to sit on your lap while you drive that tractor."

"We're implementing a music program for every Friday night. We still have a few open dates. Can I sign us up?"

"I think I'd rather be in India." And she snuggled her head under my chin. I couldn't stand it any longer, and I leaned forward to kiss her. As the kisses became more intense, I reached beneath her turtleneck and found her breasts. No bra. So natural, so free! I couldn't believe my good fortune. It wasn't long before I stood up, took the sleeping bag, and arranged it on the ground. Then I reached into her pack for a blanket in case it got cold. Abby stood up too. She glanced around slowly in a 360-degree circle. I smiled as I watched her because I knew exactly what was going through her mind. Satisfied, she took off her clothes, placed them on the rock, and smiled at me as she walked over to the sleeping bag and laid down.

"Is it time to talk history again?" I asked laughing.

"Not until you get your clothes off." I hurried to comply, placing my clothes beside hers on the rock. Upon returning, I found her lying on her side. I knelt down beside her and began rubbing her back.

"I love you Abby. You are really precious and so beautiful." She slowly turned onto her back and looked at me fighting back tears.

"I love you too, Jeff. You are the best thing that has happened to me in a long, long time. I love your integrity, your commitment to living an authentic life, and you are so talented and handsome." And she smiled up at me for the first time. "And we enjoy doing all these simple things—making love in an open meadow and sleeping in a tent in a Greek temple."

"With me, it was more simple," and I gently stroked her body from her neck on down. "It hit me at the auction almost immediately. I was blown away. Only later did I learn that I had fallen for a bright, playful, caring woman. And now that's it for talking," and I fell on top of her.

"Thank goodness. You're finally making some sense." We made love for almost an hour as we slowly explored our connected bodies. Time stood still as we shared this God given gift of passion and love.

Afterward she got up from the sleeping bag and opened a bottle of wine. "Just one glass each," she said as she rejoined me. "We need to save the rest for tonight." After a brief pause while she sipped the wine, she asked: "Do you know anything about Tantrism?"

"Yes, it's a Buddhist sect," I replied.

"A Buddhist sect where people believe the road to the divine is through lovemaking. Want to join?" she asked with a playful grin.

"I'm not sure they allow physical love to proceed to orgasm. It's my understanding they use sexual arousal to get their combined creative energies flowing but stop short of orgasm. But I could be wrong."

"Forget that," she said with a laugh. "We'll have to create our own sect."

"Will there be any rules or obligations?"

"I don't know about the rules yet, but there is one obligation," she said as she sipped her wine and smiled over at me.

"What's that?" I asked.

"Only that we never lose the passion and interest of the last fifty minutes."

"I've always thought God was present when two people were making love. There's so much that's special, magical really. That's the divine part. All the magic that goes beyond the physical pleasure."

"I just thought of the first rule," she said as she got up laughing and took the two wine glasses and placed them in her pack.

"What's that?" I asked as I looked over at her smiling.

"When my clothes are off, there's to be no minister talk."

"I think I can manage that." When I finally put my watch on along with the rest of my clothes, it was three thirty in the afternoon. With a lightened load and a new skip to our beat, we started on our way to Delphi.

*   *   *

To get to Delphi from the meadow, you circle back toward the house. That part of the trip took thirty minutes. It was a pleasant walk because we were headed west into a warm sun. It was up one knoll and down another all over again. The trees with their budding leaves could be seen in the distance.

There's an old burned-out barn along the way. All that remains is the rock foundation and some planks, but it provided an attractive place to sit for a few minutes. It wasn't that we needed to rest, particularly, but I wanted to sit and watch the sun go down over the western peaks. I love the extended twilight period made possible by these peaks because it usually is a time of calm and peace.

"There's beauty everywhere," Abby said as I helped her up onto the foundation. "How much time do we have left to reach your temple?"

"No more than twenty-minutes."

"Good. That gives us plenty of time before we start losing light provided I don't get a sermon," she said as she took my hand and squeezed it. "I do have a question, however."

"Make it simple."

"This isn't simple, just really scary. I got a call last week from my best friend in high school who was diagnosed with stage four breast cancer. She's having a mastectomy this Thursday. Her long-term prospects sound rather iffy to me."

"That does sound scary, and really sad."

"She has two cute kids, a boy and a girl, who are a little younger than the twins."

"What's the husband like? She's really going to need him."

"I agree, and I'm not sure about that. I don't really know him that well. But here's what this is all about. My first instinct was to pray. I prayed that night asking God to cure her disease. The next day I began wondering if I was wasting my time. Does God intervene to heal disease?"

"I don't find any evidence for it. I preached a sermon on it once and referred to the holocaust. Six million Jews prayed to the same God you did last week, and no Jews were rescued. With regard to diseases like cancer, many Christians earnestly pray for God to intervene. Some of these victims survive and some do not. I believe in a God of love, and I can't imagine such a God would pick and choose."

"I guess I really agree with that. Do you pray?"

"Yes, I do, although many Christians would not recognize it as such. There's a wonderful Trappist monk named Thomas Keating who has written a lot on the subject. He defines prayer as practicing the presence of God. According to Keating, humans become aware of God's presence in silence. He recommends that you sit in a comfortable place, close your eyes, and work to quiet your mind by ignoring the myriad thoughts that float through it. When you get good at this practice, love floats through your awareness."

"Is it hard?"

"Not really. It just takes practice. I have one of his books at home which you can take back to Durham if you're interested."

"Is it like meditation?"

"Yes, in many ways. Keating was very much influenced by Buddhism. The whole question of prayer hinges on how one sees God working in the world. Does God intervene directly in human lives and the natural world? That's the biblical view.

"For me, God operates in a far more subtle way. We say God is love. What does that mean? God cannot be defined, only sensed as goodness and love. Keating says this goodness and love is encountered in silence. Martin Buber says that we encounter the love of God when two people relate to one another as thous, rather than its, when we see each other as the other wants to be seen.

"Buber makes the important point that the love encountered is not within the person but in the realm of the between. I see myself as a biological being through and through."

"I've noticed that, and I know just the right buttons to push."

"You're impossible."

"I know, so get back to it. You're keeping me in suspense. I'm dying to know what is this between."

"It's the social space between two individuals. Love is not within a person, but all around. It is encountered when two people mutually care about each other. Once I encounter this love, it changes my inner world in ways that help me move away from self-centered concerns. The fact that this love exists outside of my biological existence is important because it points to God. It would be hard to make an argument for God if this love was located within the person.

"Now, let me make one final point about all of this, and we're done. I'm sorry about this Sweetheart, but you have gotten me all wound up."

"That's okay. We'll soon have wine for unwinding."

"That sounds wonderful, but here's the point. God is not a being who interjects himself into the natural order to change some outcome, but rather the source of the goodness and love one encounters in every day living. True religion is about living this love. There's actually a message to it. When your mind is flooded with love, new thoughts emerge. The point is to act on them. What religion is not about is the idea that by affirming Jesus as your savior you are guaranteed a place in heaven."

"The salvation myth. That was a nice sermon," she said as she squeezed my hand.

"Sometimes you get lucky."

"I would say in your case that happens more than sometimes," she said as she winked at me while releasing my hand. "I think I will take you up on Keating's book."

"It's an easy read." And then after a brief pause: "Ready to go?"

"I've been excited to see this temple ever since you told me about it in Durham."

"I hope I haven't hyped it too much," I said as I took her hand to help her off the timbers that made up the old foundation.

"Everything is hyped about religion if you ask me."

"That's really a profound statement which we'll leave for another time. It's the problem with religious experience. It's subtle, but people have a real tendency to exaggerate their own encounters."

"Why leave it? It's my turn to be profound," Abby said as she released my hand.

"Six months ago you preferred mystery."

"Good point. I'll settle for profound mystery."

"Now we're back to God," I said laughing as I took her hand again and pulled her onto the path.

"That's okay as long as you're talking about a she."

"What if we think of God in Tillich's conception as the ground of being?"

"How do you talk to a ground of being?"

"In silence, according to Keating."

"So I have to become a Trappist monk. There goes your whoopie, my friend."

"I better teach you another way to pray."

"Just keep me off of my knees. They're already taking on a rather knobby look," she said as she dropped my hand and jumped on ahead.

"In five minutes, take the path to the right," I called out. Abby led the way along an old path through a woods of oak, hickory, locust, and popular trees with a few hemlocks wedged between. It was thick, and unfortunately was blocking the sun which lent a distinctive chill to the air. Abby briefly interrupted her progress to put on a heavy sweater, which allowed me to catch up. Ten minutes later we emerged into a small clearing. All that was left was to climb a steep hill to the top of the ridge and look over.

The mountaintops came together in a 360-degree circle. Abby recognized it immediately. "This is it," she said as she took my hand and looked down into my temple. "You've got a little tent down there."

"I come here often. I put the tent up on Friday."

"Is that a rock fireplace in the middle?"

"I built it two years ago. See all the wood beside it. I collected it after putting the tent up. We'll need the wood. I expect it will get quite cold tonight."

"The place is incredible. You didn't hype it at all. Not exactly what I pictured when you described it to me, but incredible nonetheless."

"The great thing is that I've never seen anyone for miles. I think of it as my own oasis." I took her hand, and we started our descent slowly down the steep incline.

*   *   *

Upon arriving at our campsite, I let go of her hand and moved toward the fire pit. "You can leave your pack on the little table and look around. I'll start the fire."

"Is it five o'clock somewhere?" she asked as she lifted her pack from her shoulders." I quickly looked down at my watch.

"Five-thirty according to my watch."

"I'll get the wine out." After a brief pause, "I see you brought cheese and crackers. I'll bring them too. Sipping wine by the fire: it doesn't get better than that." She enjoyed feeding the fire. "It's a shame the twins never got into girl scouts. I would have enjoyed being a leader."

"You can teach them camping skills this summer."

"In between tennis camp," and she winked over at me.

"We have to make summer plans, and I have some news."

"Oh, dear God. I need more wine."

"It's good news, I think. Pretty soon after you guys left in February, I was at Woodlands, and this woman came up to me after one of my sets. She's in charge of the West Wind Cruise Lines sales office in Florida, and she offered me a job."

"You're kidding."

"Actually she wasn't in a position to offer me a job, but she said her company was in need of good entertainers. Would I be interested? I asked for more details, and she said that every contract was different, but that I would start with a free cruise and a small stipend. I said sure I was interested, and I gave her my name, address, and phone number.

"To shorten the story, a week later Gunilla Sjostrand called from Sweden and offered me the job. I'll be performing on the Sea Cloud beginning on June 12th. The cruise is for fourteen days. We start in Rome, end up in Athens with three days in the Holy Land."

"What about your park job? You'll be leaving at a busy time."

"My job is changing there too. You may not have met Holly Pritchard. She's a third-grade teacher at the Valle Crucis school who is retiring in June. She was looking for a part-time job, and we worked out a deal to share the job. The only problem is that I'm leaving on the 10th which doesn't give me much time to show her the ropes.

"But here's the real point. Will you come with me? I get a cabin with the crew, and I'm allowed a companion."

"Wow, that sounds like fun, but you're not giving me much notice."

"I know. The whole thing only came into place last week. Originally we were looking at a cruise from Puerto Rico up the Amazon in early September, but I got a call from Gunilla about ten days ago asking me if I could do the one in June too. I'll be substituting for a guy who's going home to visit his parents. His mother is dying of cancer."

"I'll do my best. It really does sound like fun. I've never been to the Holy Land, and Rome is one of my favorite places."

"We could leave a few days early for Rome if you want."

"Let's deal with first things first. I'll talk to Gar as soon as I get home. As I told you this afternoon, he wants to make a trip to India before the baby is born to see his extended family and was planning to go sometime this summer. Maybe I can talk him into going in June and taking the twins with him."

"That would be great. I may be pushing my luck here; but if you come, I would love to share the stage with you. I don't need you up there, but it feels so good when you are." Abby got out from her seat around the fire and came to join me on the other side. She put her arms around me, and buried her head against my shoulder. She squeezed hard, and then lifted her chin to face me. In a whisper, she said:

"Jeff, I am not an entertainer. I don't really like being the center of attention, and yet I'm going to admit something to you. When you smiled at me that first time I was on the stage at Woodlands, I melted. When the girls were so proud of me in January, it felt good. I'm amazed I'm not really nervous up there. You make it easy. So sure. I can join you off and on if this little junket works out."

"You're the best Abby. You make me sound so much better," and I kissed her long and tenderly.

"I hope I add something, but we're going to have a little contract, you and me."

"Name your terms."

"I will join you on stage off and on, but I don't want to be a permanent fixture. We're a couple, not a singing duo. I also want to be able to take a night off if something good comes up."

"Those terms are easy. You have a deal. Do we kiss on it or just shake hands?"

"Well you just kissed me. How about you get dinner. I'm starved."

"I've got four chicken salad sandwiches for us to share, potato chips, two oranges, and there's more wine."

"You know Jeff. I don't think you can afford to share that salary with that third-grade teacher."

"Why do you say that?"

"Because you lavish so much money on me it's ridiculous."

"I certainly am a proponent of simple living."

"As I've said before, some girls have all the luck," she said as she got up from the fire, and started walking toward my little table. "I'll get our dinner. It's girl's work. You keep me warm tonight."

We sipped wine, fed the fire, ate dinner, and she told me funny stories about the twins. At some point in the evening, I totally lost track of the time, Abby squeezed my thigh and used my shoulder to lift herself from the ground. "It's time for bed. I'm going off to pee. You do what you need to do, and maybe you ought to make the fire safe."

I walked off in the opposite direction. When she returned, she began collapsing the tent. "I see we're not sleeping in the tent," I said as I looked over at her. I was kneeling by the fire, centralizing it so that it would not spread during the night.

"Why sleep in a tent when we can sleep under the stars? If it rains, which I sincerely doubt, we'll just get wet. We'll use the tent for ground cover." I watched her prepare the bed with the efficiency of an expert camper and thought she really had missed her calling as a Girl Scout leader. When she finished, she walked to the little wooden table and took off her shoes, jeans, and heavy sweater. She climbed into the sleeping bag in her socks, panties, turtleneck, and a light sweater.

"You're going to freeze, Abby," I said as I completed the job of securing the fire.

"Not with you in here beside me, and you're only invited if you take your clothes off too. I want to feel strong, hairy, masculine legs keeping me warm, not scratchy, dirty jeans. "

I did as I was told and climbed in beside her. It took a little wiggling around to get things straightened out, but it was fun. We wrapped our arms around each other and hugged tightly to get warm. It felt so good to be enclosed in this wonderful woman, I thought as I closed my eyes and strengthened my grip. When we finally separated, she rested her head on the pillow (our extra blanket) and gazed at the stars. I buried my head against her shoulder, and my left hand reached under her turtleneck and found her breasts. I couldn't keep myself away from her.

I was content to hold her in silence, but she wanted to talk about the stars. "You're missing a spectacular show."

"I'm so comfortable. Tell me about it."

"I'm just thinking about the huge distances that separate us and all that open space up there."

"Jews living in first century Palestine thought the distance was quite short and that God used the stars as windows to spy on people from heaven. If you planned to sin, it was best to do it on a cloudy night when God wouldn't see you."

"Then you better remove your hand, pal, 'cuz God's got you nailed."

"Not if my God's male. He's lovin' it."

"You guys always find a way to get away with it."

"What if she's female?" I asked.

"She'd surprise a lot of fundamentalists." I gripped Abby tightly and hugged her. "Can you name the constellations for me?" I asked.

"I was trying to figure that out before you sidetracked me with that peeping Tom stuff. Let's see. There's Pegasus, the winged horse. I looked for him first because he sort of orients me. Right below him is Lyra. I can always find her because of the four stars that make a square. Above Pegasus is Pisces. I think I have him, but he really doesn't look much like a fish. To the right of Pegasus is Taurus, the Bull, and then there's Orion. He's always easy to find."

"Wow! You know your stuff."

"The raw material of poetry. But reflecting on the meaning of it is more important. I get goose bumps just thinking about how it works. We are so tiny in all this vastness."

"I know what you mean. You and I lie on solid ground, the sun will rise tomorrow as it always does, and yet this tiny planet is flying around in a vast space."

"Life is so precious," she responded. "Do you know what's so great about being out here, Jeff?"

"What's that?" I replied.

"To be in nature, to be a part of it and not closed off from it or to view it from some protected haven. That's what's so special. I could write terrific poetry here."

"What would you write about?"

"I would write about the stars and human intimacy, about the mystery and the beauty of good sex, about six-sided houses, and churches in the woods. About all the experiences that provide life with richness and meaning. This is going to be so perfect."

"You know, maybe I could do a little writing too."

"I'm a good editor. What would you write about?"

"One issue that burns in me is the relationship between revelation and belief. When one reaches out to another, the experience of love and goodness can be overwhelming, but it has no content. Humans invent the content out of which comes religious doctrine. The human mind is a very powerful tool for defining experience and unfortunately for deception. All religious doctrine suffers from this problem."

"That's an ambitious topic."

"I know. So let's change the subject." After a brief pause, I hugged her tight and said: "You know, you're a very silly girl."

"I know. It used to drive Gar crazy."

"I love it. Opposites must attract. I get so hung up on big ideas, so serious at times. You lighten me up. It's wonderful."

"That's so nice, Jeff," and she returned my hug. "Listen: while we're on the topic of lightening up, let me excuse myself and go outside for one more pee. That wine was insidious." And she wiggled her way out of the sleeping bag and ran off into the night. A few minutes later she came running back, wiggled her way back in beside me and said: "Hold me, Jeff. I'm freezing." She wrapped her arms around me and buried her head in my neck.

128

A short time afterward she lifted her head and whispered in my ear. "Can you keep a secret?"

"I'm quite good at that."

"Especially from my Chapel Hill friends."

"I may never see them again."

"Good point. You're safe then. I may be a little different from my Chapel Hill friends. I like to be led as long as the man is gentle and kind. It's like dancing. I like following a good male dancer. I'm learning to enjoy singing on stage because I work with such a talented, handsome lead singer. I love to be silly with a man who truly loves me and who is strong enough to take good natured teasing. You are truly a good man Jeff. You've had some tough personal issues and you've come out so strong."

"Thanks Abby, but it was probably easier for me. I was healthy psychologically before all the shit happened. Chemical depression can be so much harder to recover from. I had the blues, not deep- seated psychological problems caused by chemical issues in my brain."

"That may be true, but here you go again. You are so honest about yourself. That's a real sign of psychological strength."

"I love you Abby."

"I love you too Jeff, and I can feel that love. It's making me all warm inside." She moved her head slightly for one last kiss and was soon asleep. This time it was my turn to gaze at the stars. Sleep did not come quickly. It rarely did, especially on that hard ground, but I was in no hurry. The warmth of her body, the gentle rhythm of her breathing, and the thought that God was keeping this magical spot from spinning out of control into a cold, dark universe produced a peace in me that passed all understanding. I am a very lucky man, I thought as sleep finally won over.

Chapter 10

The Sea Cloud

ABBY AND I FLEW from Charlotte to New York City and from there to Rome on June 10th. The cruise was for two weeks, and Gar was thrilled to have the twins. He took them to India for a month.

West Wind was cooperative too. I was originally scheduled to be given a cabin with the crew, at the waterline with no veranda. I gave up my small stipend in exchange for a stateroom with a veranda. I figured I owed Abby a good view. We were placed on deck 6.

Our work at the Whale's Tail was routine—much like what I did at Woodlands. We were scheduled to perform from 8:30 to 10:30 every night. The Whale's Tail was a bar, with a small stage, and comfortable seating for about sixty people.

Abby was the real employee for West Wing from our duo. She sang with me off and on, but she was always there visiting with guests when not on stage. I called them Abby's groupies—regular guests who became our friends. They came from all over the world, many with distinguished careers and interesting backgrounds. We kept up with a few of them for many years.

Because we worked at night, we were free to go on several memorable excursions. The tour of ancient Rome was one of the best with the Colosseum, the Arch of Constantine, the Roman Forum, and the imposing Palatine Hill. We also visited several Greek islands. I was most impressed with the medieval village in the Old Town of Rhodes. We learned all about the history of Minoan Civilization at the Heraklion Archaeological Museum on the island of Crete.

But our big day was in Jerusalem. We landed at the Israeli port of Haifa on the sixth day of the cruise. The next day we toured Nazareth and the Sea of Galilee which was a little disappointing. Nazareth was a bust. It's an Arab city with few traces of the historical Jesus. The Sea of Galilee gave me goose bumps as I pictured Jesus speaking in the rolling fields that surround this picturesque lake. The seaside village of Capernaum, the center of the Jesus movement during his lifetime, was an archeological gem with important remains of Peter's mother-in-law's house and an ancient synagogue in which Jesus may have spoken. We also went to a site along the Jordan River where Jesus was allegedly baptized by John the Baptist. It was nothing more than a tourist trap.

But Jerusalem was the best—a stunning and an amazing place. We left the ship at 7:15 in the morning for what was to become a very long day. The bus ride to the city that has played such a prominent role in the history of the three great monotheistic religions was a little more than two hours. I was expecting Abby to talk about some of the important monuments we would soon see, but she had work on her mind.

"I was talking with that cute blond singer from Croatia last night, and she has a three-month contract. How come yours is only for two weeks?"

"I thought I explained. I'm only substituting on this cruise. The guy I'm replacing asked for some time off to be with his mother who is dying of pancreatic cancer."

"You're right. I do remember something like that when we were drinking wine at your temple. But what happens in September?"

"I told West Wind I could only work for a month at a time, and then I needed two months off."

"Did they agree?"

"They booked me for September, although that may depend on how we do on this cruise."

"Maybe I should sing off key." And she paused and took my hand. "I guess I can live with that. These cruises are fun, but they will take you away from home."

"We'll do it one cruise at a time. We can bring the twins with us next summer."

"That would be nice," Abby said as she gave my right hand a squeeze. And then after pausing again, "Maybe I should be quiet so we can pay more attention to our tour guide."

"That depends on what's on your mind."

"Well it doesn't make sense to talk about Tantric blessings. That's one religion they haven't heard about in Jerusalem."

"To their great loss, but listen up Sweetheart. Our guide is talking about all the Muslim sites we will see on the Temple Mount. You might be interested."

"Anything is better than talking to you about sex that never gets anywhere," she said as she squeezed my hand one last time while directing her attention to the front of the bus. An hour later I became excited as the bus began its ascent up the steep Judean mountains which surround Jerusalem. Fifteen minutes later the bus backed into a tight parking space that provided us access to a large scenic viewing area for the Mount of Olives.

"Oh, Abby, this is magnificent. Just like all the pictures I have studied over the years. The Dome of the Rock jumps right out at you. Do you see it? It's right in the middle of the Temple Mount, which was the site of the Second Temple that the Romans destroyed in 70 A.D."

"Tell me that crazy Dome of the Rock story again."

"Muhammad seems to have hopped on a winged mule in Mecca which he flew to the spot where the Dome of the Rock now sits. From there he took off again and flew to heaven with the angel Gabriel where he met God, and several Old Testament prophets. After completing these meetings, he flew home to Mecca."

"I remember studying Greek and Roman mythology in high school. That story comes from the same genre."

"Some Islamic scholars say it was a spiritual journey, a vision experience that Muhammad had."

"It's still amazing that such stories can be believed. We have our virgin birth believers too."

"And the problem is those beliefs have consequences, people fight over them, but look at this splendid city before us. Much of the Old Testament story is there. Right to the left of the Temple Mount was the city of David. God didn't allow David to build a temple because he was a bad boy, a man of war and bloodshed. As a result, God gave the task of building the first temple to David's son, Solomon. On top of the ridge on the left is where all the upper-class Jews lived in the first century. Herod's palace was somewhere in that area. Lower Jerusalem was where the poor lived. They lived in groups defined by their trade. There was a Potter's Lane, a blacksmith's street and so on. The homeless hung out right next to the dump which was located in that lower left-hand corner over there," and I pointed out the general direction.

"Jeff," she whispered while gently nudging me. "Our group seems to be heading back to the bus."

"That means we're on our way to Gethsemane, Sweetheart. Do you see those green trees right in front of the Temple Mount? That's it." The bus ride to the garden of Gethsemane was a little less than ten minutes down a steep, windy, narrow mountain road.

"I'm glad you're not driving," Abby said as she playfully poked me with her elbow.

"Me too," I said as I took her hand. The bus parked along a side street which left us with a five minute walk into the garden where Jesus was arrested not quite 2,000 years ago.

"It's beautiful," Abby said as we slowly walked among wild flowers and a grove of olive trees.

"Let's break off from the group. I see a nice rock we can sit on across the way over there," and I pointed. "I have no interest in hearing another account of Jesus's arrest." Much to my relief she willingly took my hand, and we headed for the rock.

When we were both seated on the rock, I gently raised her chin so that she was looking directly at me. "Okay, my best friend who has become the love of my life. I have a serious question to ask. Will you marry me?"

"Oh, my God, Jeff. How could I say no in this beautiful garden? Two years ago I never wanted to get married again. After that night we spent in the woods, I've been waiting for this day with my fingers crossed. You're the best thing that has happened to me in as long as I can remember. Yes, yes, yes," and she moved closer to kiss me passionately.

"Nice things can happen in this garden too," I said as I reached into my pocket for the ring. I took her left hand and slipped it onto the appropriate finger. She was speechless, an Abby I had never seen before. She gazed at the ring, and then looked back at me.

"It's so beautiful, Jeff," and there were tears in her eyes. "I just can't believe this is all happening. I will never forget this lovely garden."

"I love you Abby."

"I love you too," and we kissed passionately one last time.

"Jeffie," Abby sheepishly whispered up at me. "I think we are creating quite a scene for our fellow travelers, and you're a West Wind employee."

"Have you ever heard of the Gospel of Mary? It's a Gnostic gospel. You would have loved the Gnostics."

"You can tell me all about them later."

"In the Gospel of Mary, there's one scene where Jesus is necking with Mary in the woods. He takes her hand and leads her away from a group of their companions just like I did."

"But he was the son of God. That gave him lots of cover. You're nothing but a lowly entertainer."

"And you're nothing but a guest."

"That's what makes it so dangerous. Remember Patrick Swayze in "Dirty Dancing?" He lost his job for doing it with a guest."

"I don't remember his losing his job. It's that last dance that sticks in my mind."

"I'm not surprised," she whispered up at me with a grin. "She was all tits and ass."

"And you're not cut from the same cloth?"

"Jeffie, please. I'm an engaged lady."

"That's what makes you so special, Sweetheart," and I kissed her one last time. "But maybe you're right," and we made our way back to the group. Because the group seemed to be in no hurry to move on, Abby quietly asked:

"Is there a story that goes with this ring?"

"Sort of. My grandmother had a broach with five diamonds which she gave to Brenda when she was a little girl. Brenda used one for her engagement ring, and was happy to give you this one."

"I can't wait to meet her."

"She's looking forward to meeting you too. The sapphires were my contribution."

"It's so beautiful Jeff," she said as she took my hand as we headed back to the bus. With the most important part of the day behind me, I relaxed and enjoyed the rest of the tour. We visited the old city with its narrow, cobblestone streets and bustling bazaars. "It's amazing Jeff. Arabs and Jews are living so closely together."

"The sections of the city are segregated, but you're right. They all run into each other."

"It's so stupid. God has made special promises to all three groups, and it's the same God, and all they can do is fight."

"It's the best example of what is wrong with religion. The focus is all on ideological belief, and not the love that this shared God bestows on all of them. Not to change the subject, but we're approaching the wailing wall. The Jews you see praying there are mostly Orthodox with their beards and elaborate costumes."

"Where did the name wailing wall come from?"

"When the Romans destroyed the Second Temple in 70 A.D., only a small section of the wall remained on this west side. The ground of the Temple Mount is sacred land for Jews. When the UN divided Jerusalem in 1948 between the new state of Israel and Jordan, this entire area was held by Jordan. The result was that Jews could only gaze on this wall from a distance and wail. This all changed when Israel defeated Jordan in the 1967 war and took control of this area."

"It's all about stupid beliefs as you were saying."

"We're just about to add the Christian component. This beautiful church we are approaching is called the Church of the Holy Sepulchre. It's an amazing place with awe inspiring frescos, and several chapels which claim to document the New Testament story of Jesus's crucifixion, burial, and resurrection."

"Do you believe that stuff?" Abby whispered up at me as we entered the church holding the admission tickets our guide had handed us.

"Not really, Sweetheart," I whispered back. "For one thing historians are pretty convinced there was no burial. It was Roman policy to leave victims on the cross after they died to be devoured by animals. They wanted the punishment to be so horrible it would act as a deterrent for anyone thinking about causing political trouble."

"How could there have been a resurrection then?" she asked as we moved toward the back of the church and leaned against an outside wall. "There would have been no body to fly up to heaven."

"No physical resurrection as the gospels describe, but Paul had a different view. He met the resurrected Jesus in a vision experience he had on the Damascus road. Jesus was sitting at the right hand of God. His spiritual body had risen to join God in heaven, but we've been over this before. I'm just repeating myself."

"Do you believe Paul's version of the story?"

"It's certainly easier than the physical version."

"I may prefer the physical version," Abby whispered back to me. "Thinking of that beautiful man being devoured by animals is disgusting."

"There's no question about his being a beautiful man," and I took her hand as we followed our group into the chapel that commemorates his burial. When the tour of the church ended, we walked with our guide through the Muslim quarter of the city, most of which had been destroyed in the '67 war and has been rebuilt with authentic stone. Again, it was through narrow cobblestone streets, another thriving bazaar, and eventually through the Damascus gate which took us out of the old city. Our bus was waiting about three blocks away.

The rest of our tour involved a late lunch at a five-star hotel, a bus tour of the new city, and the two-hour trip back to the ship. I would have loved to see the West Bank and all those settlements, but this was not part of the tour plan. Our Jewish guide was uncomfortable even talking about the settlement issue as was evident in his response to a question from one of the members of our group. Abby nestled her head against my shoulder and slept most of the way back to the ship.

*   *   *

I woke up at my usual time of 6:30 a.m., the day following our exciting trip to Jerusalem, showered, shaved, and took the few required steps from the bathroom to the dresser I shared with Abby in our tiny cabin. My plan was to go to deck 7 where they had a coffee café that served a continental breakfast and plenty of comfortable chairs providing views of the ocean.

Today was a sea day. We were traveling from the port at Haifa to the Greek island of Rhodes at the point where the Mediterranean becomes the Aegean Sea. A sea day was a day to relax on the ship. We had plans to attend a lecture on the unfolding of the Big Bang by a former top executive of NASA and to walk for an hour on the second deck which had a quarter mile track that circled the ship.

As I looked at the mirror above the dresser, I saw Abby stretching in our bed. "You're up early, Babe. Did you sleep well?"

"Not really."

"Everything okay."

"Everything's fine. My mind was just racing."

"I'm on my way to my favorite spot on deck 7," I said while pulling up my pants. "Come join me."

"I can't eat all those donuts and fancy muffins. I'll get a plate of scrambled eggs and see you there."

"Great," I said while lacing my running shoes. I was soon able to walk around the bed and give her a big kiss. "You're so beautiful, Sweetheart. I'm the luckiest guy ever."

"You might even get luckier," she said yawning and then smiling up at me. "If you get me a cup of coffee, we can make a little whoopie before breakfast. There's no rush. We have no deadlines to meet today."

"I'll be back in five minutes."

It took a little longer to get to deck 7 than I had originally planned. When we finally arrived there, we got great window seats on a comfortable soft leather sofa. There was quite a wind outside which made the sea interesting to watch.

But Abby had no interest in watching the ocean. "When Gar and I were married, he would invariably call a meeting whenever there were plans to be made. So I'm calling our first meeting to order. I slept fitfully last night cuz I was making plans."

"About what?"

"Wedding plans dummy," and she jabbed me in the side. "Women's work primarily, but you need to have a say."

"I have quite a lot of experience with weddings."

"Not like the one I have in mind."

"This ought to be good."

"I'm certainly too old to walk down the aisle in a white dress. What I want to do is get married at Luther's Rock."

"It won't be a big wedding."

"Just three of us. You, me, and Father Greg. After we're married, we'll have a big party at the Apple Barn to celebrate."

"I like it."

"We don't need to have the party on the same day as the ceremony. We can do the ceremony before. That rock is a special place for me. It was when I really started thinking you were a pretty cool guy."

"What about the timing?"

"I was thinking October. Is that too soon for you?"

"Good timing, our first anniversary."

"I'm so excited, Jeff," and she took my hand and squeezed it. "This couldn't be better for us. The twins start high school in the fall. They would be starting a new school in Durham. This will make the transition so much easier. Moving to Beaver Dam at the end of July will work out well."

"Schools in Watauga county start early in August. So you can move sooner if that would help."

"We'll see about that as the summer progresses."

"The one thing I have heard about our schools is that they are generally pretty good. The high school in particular has a good reputation."

"I have heard that too. Actually the girls will be thrilled to move to Boone. They'll think of it as one big skiing vacation."

"The one thing that may have to go is our cruise work. I don't want to be leaving you guys for extended periods of time."

"That probably is a good idea, but once the girls are out of high school we can get back to doing it again. There's a lot to be said for touring the world on West Wind."

"I can wait four years. What do you plan to do about teaching?"

"Nothing immediately. We'll have to have another meeting to discuss our combined finances, but I suspect we're in pretty good shape. If I want to go back to work after we're all settled in, I'm sure I can find something at App State."

"I think you could too. It's becoming a much better university."

"That's what my friend Judy tells me."

"I forgot about her. She can certainly help you with a job."

"We'll play all that by ear. One thing we do have to think about is housing. I'm afraid you'll find your charming little place too confining with two teenage step-daughters in residence."

"I'm afraid you're right about that. I'll talk with George to see if we can buy my place, and then we can add on. If he won't sell, we can certainly find another special place. The mountains are full of them."

"At least there's no rush. We have your place while we look into other possibilities. I can't believe this is all happening. I can't believe I'm getting married again."

"Will you be taking my name? It won't hurt my feelings if you don't."

"I'll have to think about that. Probably. I didn't take Gar's last name because it was so long and because I was trying to establish myself as a credible professional. But the circumstances are different this time. Sharing the same name is a nice symbol, and I'm somewhat traditional as you are learning." I wanted to throw my arms around her and kiss her long and hard, but we weren't alone so I behaved myself.

"Can I move that the meeting be adjourned?" I said as I squeezed her hand tightly.

"Pretty good first meeting, Bud. No arguments, no tears."

"Did Gar ever bring you to tears?"

"Only when he was hitting golf balls, but they were tears of laughter."

"I can't wait to play golf with you in the mountains. It's all up hill and down. Some of our courses are quite challenging."

"I'll give you a few strokes. I don't like beating up on guys."

"I bet you're pretty good."

"I've got a hot putter."

"Where'd you get it?"

"I stole it." She paused briefly and then got up from the sofa. "Your silly girl needs some exercise. Sixteen laps around the ship or I can't eat lunch. This place breeds calories."

"With that wind outside, we'll get lots of exercise."

*　　*　　*

Five days later we were moored off the island of Mykonos, the smallest of the Greek islands on the Aegean Sea ninety-three miles east of Athens. It is an island made famous by Jackie Onassis in the 1960s, and it was easy to see why she was so taken by it. From the veranda off of our stateroom on the ship, I focused binoculars on a beautiful beach, a string of whitewashed houses with deep blue doors, and a nineteenth century windmill far off to the right.

Abby and I left the ship at 10 a.m. for a walking tour of Chora, the main town on the island with a population of 7,000. From our tour guide we learned the white houses along the shoreline were originally owned by fishermen. The balconies of the houses were directly above the water. Abby guessed they served the same function as the nineteenth century widow walks on the coast of Massachusetts. As tourism has emerged as the major industry in Mykonos, these houses have become restaurants, bars, and gift shops.

The historic district of Chora is made up of a labyrinth of narrow lanes. We stopped at a bakery where we sampled freshly baked koulouri (a sesame bun), and then on to the Church of Panagia Paraportiani, a large white structure that, from the outside, looked more like a mosque than a Greek Orthodox church. When we arrived at the Archaeological Museum of Chora, Abby had had enough.

"We've been to enough museums on this trip, Jeff," she whispered over at me. "Let's break off from the tour and make our way back to the ship. I need to stretch my legs. This stop and go pace has left me with a large pain in my lower back."

"Fine with me. We should make it back in less than an hour. I will inform our guide of our change in plans and give her a small tip." As we headed back on our own, Abby quickly commented.

"Wouldn't it be great to spend the first few years of our married life here."

"It would certainly be expensive. I bet the rents are out of sight—especially those along the water."

"You'll be surprised what we can afford. Wait till you see the first statement from my broker. I told you Gar was very generous with the divorce settlement. He also invested my money well. There's really no need for me to work once we get to Beaver Dam. I'm in no rush to go back to the classroom. Certainly not until we're all settled and then only on an adjunct basis. And if you're a good boy, you can retire with me."

"I'll be a good boy. I'll be a good boy. I promise. Wow—Gar is definitely growing on me, but I can't leave the Park in the lurch."

"I wouldn't want you to. You can always go on the Board or help them in some other way as a volunteer. If you could do anything without the pressure to earn a living, what would that be?"

"Become a songwriter—no question about it. Making music comes from a place deep within me. I never discovered that until I came to North Carolina."

"You're a natural entertainer. I'll teach you how to write lyrics."

"No, it won't work that way. I will put your lyrics to music. We can do this together."

"You've got a deal," Abby said as she took my hand to shake it. We had come to a stop sign that marked the end of the historic part of the town. After crossing the street, we stepped up to a sidewalk that would take us to the ship which was docked a half mile ahead. Abby took my hand again, looked up at me, smiled, and continued where she had left off.

"Where will you go with your music Jeff? How high are your ambitions?"

"I've never thought about that. Until fifteen minutes ago I had thought of music as a hobby rather than a way to earn a living. However, the first thing I'm going to do is find a good classical guitar teacher. I need to improve my playing. We'll have four years while the twins are in high school for me to work on my guitar and for us to plan for a new future."

"I may spend more time writing poetry. Like you, I seem to be called in that way. Something inside is pushing me to see how far I can go with it. I'm also excited about the prospect of working with a songwriter," she said while taking my hand and squeezing it.

"New beginnings are exciting and a little scary."

"I know, but nothing ventured, nothing gained. I'm willing to take the risk."

"Me too," I said as I released her hand and reached into my pocket for the plastic card that was my ticket for boarding the ship. Abby followed right behind. I'm a lucky guy, I thought as I looked over my shoulder and smiled at her.

*   *   *

Jeff, will you call Greg sometime this weekend? The weather forecast is so much better on Monday than the rest of the week. We really need to get the ceremony behind us this week."

"Sure. I'll call him right now." It was about 4:30 on a Friday afternoon, and I was preparing an early dinner. We were taking the twins to a Watauga High School football game. They were excited about the prospect of hanging out with their new friends.

Abby was upstairs with the twins, and so I shouted out to her after getting Greg on the phone. "Abby, Greg is free at 10 on Monday, but he can't go all the way to Jefferson State Park. His day becomes crazy around lunch. He wants to do it at the Park. What do you think?"

"Damn," I heard her say from upstairs. And then, "give him a tentative yes, but I may change my mind. Where does he plan to do it?"

"Along the river."

"I guess you'll have to wear waders."

"Along the river, Sweetheart. Not in it."

"The Park may work, Jeff. The twins are nodding that they would like to attend."

"It's always good to have witnesses. I'll give him your tentative yes."

We met in the parking lot at the Park at ten o'clock on October 7, 1999—Abby and me, the twins, the Rev. Greg, and his wife Judy. Holly Pritchard had set up five chairs along the bank of the river, and was happy to join our merry band. The sun was shining brightly, adding a sparkle to the water. It was 63 degrees.

Greg gathered us all together, and I started to grab Abby's hand. Before taking it, she stepped over to Ana for a Kleenex to wipe her tears. I was touched. She returned, took my hand, and whispered up to me: "I'm glad I have two beautiful attendants with us." She then smiled at Greg, signaling that she was all set.

Greg began in a somewhat traditional way. "Ana and Tara, we are gathered here today along the banks of the beautiful Watauga River to join together your mother, Abigail Dunbar, and Jeffery Peterson in holy matrimony."

Turning to face Abby and me, he continued. "Jeff, you are a dear friend and counselor, and an important leader in our community. Abby, you provide energy and good cheer to each and every one you encounter. As a couple, your combined strengths will make a lasting contribution to the Valle Crucis community.

"I ask you now to join hands for the purpose of exchanging vows. The couple has chosen to commit themselves to each other with vows of their own making. Abby." Abby looked at me with those blue eyes sparkling.

"Jeff, my dearest friend, I promise to listen to your sermons if you will keep me warm at night. I promise to take you for richer or poorer, although I must admit I'm waiting with baited breath for the richer. I promise to grow old with you because I don't want anyone else to see my wrinkles. I make the traditional promise to obey with my fingers crossed. Finally, I promise not to be silly, but only on even numbered days. May I remind you all that today is October 7th."

"May I have the ring, please." Ana stepped forward to give her mother my ring. She took both of my hands and squeezed tight. "Jeff, I give you this ring because you are a good and decent man in every bone of your body. I give you this ring because you are the love of my life. Finally, I give you this ring as a symbol of all the goodness and love that exists between us." She slipped on the ring and kissed me tenderly.

Ana quickly called out: "Mom, you can't kiss yet." Abby smiled at her daughter and replied.

"There's an old song, Sweetheart, that I remember from my youth that speaks to this issue. It goes something like this. 'It's my party, and I'll kiss if I want to, kiss if I want to, kiss if I want to. You would kiss too if it was happening to you.'"

"Good point Mom. This is your party. You can kiss him again if you want to."

"I might just do that," and she kissed me again before smiling back at Ana. Greg then stepped forward and said.

"Jeff, it's your turn. You have a hard act to follow." I took both of Abby's hands.

"Abby, let me begin by promising never to resent the fact that you will so often steal the show. I also promise to laugh with you, to listen to your stories, and to reveal to you my deepest secrets and concerns. To Ana and Tara, I promise to be your good friend and to welcome you always to our home."

"May I have the ring, please." Tara came forward, handed me the ring, and gave me a big thumbs up.

"Abby, I give you this ring because you fill up my senses. I give you this ring because you have brought joy and laughter to my life. Finally, I give you this ring because I have never fallen in love so deeply." I threw my arms around her and kissed her tenderly.

Greg stepped forward one last time, smiled at us and said: "I guess nobody needs my permission to kiss around here. With that said, it is my great honor to pronounce you husband and wife." The twins ran up to give us both hugs. They were joined by Greg, Judy, and Holly, and then we all headed back to the parking lot.

As Abby and I walked back together, she whispered up at me: "A world of good can take place in ten minutes. It was just the ceremony I wanted."

Brenda's Song

Chapter 11

Two Lives Well Lived

I RETIRED FROM MY job as principal of the Cherry Creek Elementary School in Englewood Colorado in June of 2026 and moved to the mountains of North Carolina. My retirement came a little earlier than I had originally planned, but Daddy's health was declining. I arrived just in time to celebrate his eightieth birthday.

Congestive heart failure was the problem, the same disease that took my grandfather. Gapa was the key. Daddy had inherited a birth defect where the valves did not close completely after each heartbeat, making the heart muscle work harder to keep his blood moving. He had taken medication to alleviate the problem for most of his adult life, but the fact that his heart had to work harder slowly led to deterioration of the heart muscle. Abby encouraged me to come. She wanted me to be around for whatever remained of Daddy's life.

I purchased a three-bedroom cabin on Dutch Creek Road, about two miles from the Mast General Store, with the house sitting alongside the river. I couldn't believe it. I had to cross a little bridge to get to the house. It was an amazing privilege to sit on my porch and watch the world go by.

Sadly, I moved to Watauga County alone. Hank and I have been divorced for twelve years. He was an interesting guy. So intelligent and handsome, but he had a zipper problem which became intolerable. I do thank him for two wonderful sons, Hank Jr., age 27, and Scott, who is two years younger, and named after my brother. Hank is a lawyer for American high-tech firms in China, living in Shanghai, which makes it difficult for us to get together. He promised to return to the states when he and Marty, also a lawyer in China, have kids. We'll see if that happens. Scott, on the other hand, is easier to keep in touch with. He recently took a job as an engineer for First Solar Corporation designing solar panels. He is currently single, and is living in Santa Fe, New Mexico.

My new home on Dutch Creek is twenty minutes from Abby and Daddy's place on Hilliard Knob Lane. George Edwards sold them the lovely hexagonal house along with three acres twenty-seven years ago. They added on to the downstairs, built a bunkhouse thirty feet from the main house for the twins, but my room on the second floor with high school memorabilia on the walls and my old dresser from Concord was left untouched. Daddy had insisted on that. It's amazing to think of that beautiful setting with a formal road and three additional neighbors.

It's also amazing to think that Daddy and Abby have been married for twenty-eight years. Abby gave up her teaching position at Chapel Hill without complaint. While occasionally teaching a course at Appalachian State of particular interest to her, she has organized her life around my father, her children, her grandchildren, and writing poetry. She describes her station in life to friends as a demotion at work, but a huge promotion in life.

Abby's twins have gone their separate ways. Not long after Daddy and Abby were married, Abby's ex moved back to India to set up a software company for the health care industry. Sadly, for the most part, the twins lost their father which they handled differently. Ana resented Daddy as an intruder and so grew into womanhood without a father figure. She works for Morgan Stanley today as a securities analyst and has never married. She has had a difficult time with men.

Tara coped with the same problem by adopting Daddy. It was love at first sight for both of them. She even calls him Dad, which took me a little time to get over. What I do accept intellectually is that she is a fine young woman—a pediatrician with three kids of her own. She married her Watauga High School sweetheart who returned to his alma mater to teach eleventh grade American history and to coach the boy's football and track teams. Tara practices medicine part-time and takes care of all the injured Watauga High School athletes. In addition, she now takes care of my father, which makes me feel both lucky and a little resentful.

Now that I have you more or less caught up with my life, let me tell you about Abby and Daddy. Their journey together has been much more exciting than mine. As I just said, Abby, for the most part, left teaching after coming to Beaver Dam. Daddy left the Park job six months after they were married. He was able to talk Holly Pritchard into becoming the full-time director after promising to help with fundraising and by assuming responsibility for the Friday night concert program. He also served on the Board for seven or eight years after their cruising days were over.

During the first four years of their marriage while the twins were in high school, they set up home, hiked, camped at Delphi, and reflected on their future. In addition, Daddy played his guitar—often two or three hours a day. He took lessons from a classical guitarist at Appalachian State. Applying a classical style to sixties folk music made him quite unique within the community of folk artists.

Abby encouraged this endeavor. She was his biggest fan, and was happy to resume their performance work for West Wind Cruise Lines. For five years they traveled the world, two months on and two months at home. The twins were able to join them on two summer trips.

In the fall of their fourth year, lightening struck on a three-week river cruise from Bucharest to Amsterdam. Unbeknownst to either one of them, the program director at West Wind told an agent from Command Talent about them. Sheryl Hunt attended three of their performances on ship and signed on as their agent.

Two years later Perfect Pitch Records came out with a CD featuring original songs by Daddy with Abby's lyrics. Over the next ten years two additional CDs followed with concerts in several cities throughout the country. They actually made money on this venture, quite a bit of money to be truthful about it, with most of the profits being donated to the Park and other local Valle Crucis charities. Daddy was most proud of a five-mile walking trail they financed along the Watauga River that passed through the Park at the three-mile mark.

Abby also hit a homerun. The result was *More Than Encounters*. "More Than" is God's name. It sounded pretty lame to me when I first heard about it, but Daddy explained the name was almost biblical. When Moses asks God for his name in the burning bush story in Exodus, God responds that his name is Yahweh, "I am who I am." This name expresses the central truth about God's being. It is mystery, pure and simple. "More Than" expresses the central truth of a divine encounter.

"More Than Encounters," Abby and Daddy's book, received a prestigious award from the religious establishment. Unfortunately, I can't remember all the specifics surrounding the award, but here is the point. Daddy argues in the introduction that the God up there in heaven is dead. The tyrant who sits on a throne counting sin has to go. So does the loving

Father who answers prayer and the God of the Old Testament who controls history. Six million Jews prayed to this God from Nazi prison camps and ended up in gas chambers.

In its place is "More Than." Daddy points out that we can know nothing about who God is or where God resides. All we can know is the encounter, the sense of goodness and love, the social space where we meet something more. We know this God by sensing a reality that is more than the sum of its parts. This "More Than" is God. You don't define this God, create images to describe her, or try to understand what is essential mystery. Instead it's all about the experience of goodness and love that you sense in the core of your being.

After the introduction, Daddy analyzes twenty-five of Abby's poems. "Connor" is a poem about Abby holding her first grandchild. The objective reality is quite simple: we have a fifty-year old woman holding a sleeping baby boy. The experience of holding him that first time expressed in the poem is about so much more.

Another one of my favorites in the book is titled "Genesis Three." Daddy explains in the commentary that there are two different stories of creation in the first three chapters of Genesis. Abby meditates in the poem on the unfolding of the "Big Bang" fourteen billion years ago. I suspect the poem was written at Delphi. More importantly, the poem inspires a sense of awe and wonder—an encounter of "More Than." Daddy changed the original title of the poem to "Genesis Three," insisting it was a much-improved creation story from the two biblical versions. The poem brings the divine presence alive by reflecting on the beauty of the cosmos.

A third favorite is "As the Sun Rises." It describes a walk Abby and Daddy took through a misty fog in the early morning as the sun was rising. The poem evokes a sense of nature that gives me goose bumps. "More Than" was all around them. But I think you get the point.

Speaking of homeruns, my Dad hit one with me when he healed his relationship with my mother. My mom retired from her position as church organist at seventy-five. She had held the position for over forty years; and, in appreciation, the church gave her a big retirement party. Of course, my father insisted on attending. I say of course because it is always his instinct to heal wounded relationships, and his divorce from my mother and the Concord church were the biggest sores requiring healing in his life.

Our little family reunion worked because my father prepared my mother well in advance of his coming. He wrote her a long letter explaining his reasons for wanting to attend six months before the event and called her twice as the date drew near. Abby even decided to go. Her attendance certainly could have been awkward, but she is a classy lady. She stayed in the background most of the time, helped with party preparations, and smiled that beautiful smile that captured my father's heart thirty plus years ago.

The reconciliation gave my mother a new sense of peace. I loved the fact that she and Daddy were together again under the same roof. It was a little girl feeling, full of warmth and protection and silly hopes of getting back together, and I relished in it for the three days we were all together. My parents became friends again and have kept in contact ever since. My mother is still vibrant, active, and completely independent in her little house in Concord at age eighty-five. Best of all she spends at least a month with me each summer sitting on the porch soaking up the quiet magic of Dutch Creek.

In a similar manner, Daddy made his peace with the Episcopal church. One afternoon not long after my retirement while walking in the Park, I broached the subject: "I see that you and Abby have become members of Holy Cross."

"Being an Episcopalian is in my DNA, Sweetheart."

"Any second thoughts about the salvation myth? Wasn't that why you left in the first place?"

"Nope. I still see it as myth. Many Episcopalians agree with me on that issue now. There is even talk among church leaders of reexamining the creeds."

"Do you recite them on Sunday?"

"No. I close my eyes and take Abby's hand. Love usually fills my heart. It's a great replacement for them, don't you think?"

"Anything is better than reciting that old-fashioned stuff."

"The real key is focus. I wouldn't be attending if the central focus of Holy Cross centered around personal salvation. That's such a self-centered way of seeing religion. It's all about me, me, me. But that's not the case. The church is truly about helping others, about pushing the agenda of social and economic justice forward, and it's about inclusion. Most people I know at Holy Cross are committed in their own way to working on such problems, to making the world a better place. I'm really proud of the distance most members have come in the last twenty-five years."

While most of this was going on I was in Colorado, but my job allowed me to spend a month each summer with them. It was during one of those summers, about five years before my retirement, that I met Dr. Brad Sumners, a political science professor at Appalachian State with a specialty in international relations. We carried on a long-distance relationship until my retirement in 2026. Brad moved in with me in July of that year. I now have someone to hold my hand as we watch the sparkling water from Dutch Creek float by our log cabin home.

Chapter 12

Conversations on the Edge of Eternity

I LOST DADDY FIVE years after retiring and coming to North Carolina. They were five fun-filled years. There were many walks in the Park. They began as slow strolls with several stops along the way. Over time he needed a walker and then a wheelchair. Our last one required portable oxygen. I spent most of the time pushing the wheelchair fighting back tears. Propelling an obviously tired and frail old man, a prisoner to his oxygen tank, a mere shadow of the man I had loved and admired all of my life, was not an easy thing for me to do.

We also shared many meals together, and he was a big fan of Brad which made family dinners so much easier. We attended concerts together at the Park, and special functions pertaining to the Valle Crucis community. When the boys were here, they would take him fishing, they with rods and an assortment of flies, he with his chair and a book. He told me once that he spent most of his time marveling at what great kids they were.

I also loved my girl time with Abby which was to continue for the next fifteen years. We shopped, and walked, and gossiped. I also attended many grandkid events with her, mostly sporting events involving Tara's children. Over time we became great friends. As everyone who knows her will tell you, she is a class act. She had the good sense not to try to be my mother or big sister, nor was she ever territorial with Daddy despite the obvious fact that she loved him so completely.

But sadly, we have come to the point in the story when Daddy is dying. Abby gave him a special present for his seventieth birthday—a trip to China and Tibet. The Dalai Lama held a special place in Daddy's heart. Unfortunately, that heart failed toward the end of the trip in Beijing. He was lucky to survive the attack. As my discussion of our walks together at the Park suggest, the function of his heart deteriorated in plateau-like stages over those last five years. The end came on September 17, 2031.

His last week was special, however, because of two conversations that took place. The first was when I was alone with Daddy on Saturday, the ninth. The weather cooperated to some extent, but it was a little blustery. By dressing Daddy warmly, a task that Abby performed with routine nonchalance but one I never became comfortable with, and by covering his legs in a blanket, we were able to sit outside on their beautiful deck for more than two hours. The conversation was stimulating. In fact, it was quite amazing.

We talked about sports, Abby, and Mom, at my insistence. He seemed to be worried about Mom, but I kept reassuring him that she was fine. When I asked him if he had any regrets, he thought I was asking about his life generally. "Oh, a few, maybe," he said as he shifted in his wheelchair and adjusted the nose piece that delivered the oxygen. "One is that Abby and I never made the Ed Sullivan Show."

"He was long dead when you two came along."

"Maybe so, but what a voice she has! We made such great music together."

"I know, and then there was that book you wrote with her."

"One of my finest accomplishments."

"Are you afraid, Daddy?" Again he misunderstood my poorly stated question. I was wondering about his attitude toward his disease. He thought I was asking about dying. There probably wasn't much difference between the two questions. In responding, he didn't hesitate or flinch.

"No, Sweetheart," he said as he looked over at me with a broad grin on his face. "There's a part of me that looks forward to it. Many years ago I preached a sermon on death in which I suggested that life is like walking up the gentle slope of a country road. Death is the bend in that road at the top of the hill. From the perspective of walking up the hill, it is impossible to see what lies on the other side. Right now I'm only a few steps from the top of the hill. It won't be long before I can see into the other side."

"That's not exactly what I was asking about, Daddy," I said as tears welled up inside me.

"Well, I'm glad you brought it up because I would like to talk about it," he said as he fumbled for my left hand. "The only other person I have shared this with is Abby. There's a small part of all this that relates to your mother, but to understand that part, you'll have to hear the full story." He knew that lead in would peak my interest. He was clever about such things.

"I have no other plans for the afternoon," I said as I squeezed his bony, thin, hand.

"Good, and I'm here until you push me somewhere else. Do you remember Abby's gift to me when I turned seventy?"

"Yes, she gave you a trip to Tibet."

"That's right, but it ended prematurely in Beijing when I had that first heart attack. I guess it was a pretty severe attack because I almost died in our hotel room. The amazing thing was the experience that resulted from the attack. I had what psychologists call a near death experience. Have you ever heard of such a thing?"

"Vaguely," I replied as I looked over at him and smiled. "I guess we're about to embark on an exciting intellectual journey."

"No, a spiritual one, Sweetheart. It was the most incredible thing that has ever happened to me. I had just left the bathroom after shaving and all of a sudden I had this crushing pain in my chest. I collapsed on the floor. Soon afterward, I experienced this floating sensation as my consciousness literally drifted away from my body. I watched from above as Abby frantically spoke to the desk clerk of the hotel, and then I left the room on what seemed like a journey to another world."

"This is wonderful science fiction, Daddy," I said in a voice full of playful irreverence. I was enjoying his story immensely because his animated tone made me forget about all his disabilities.

"This is the core of the spiritual journey, Sweetheart. Unfortunately, you're in for a sermon," he said sheepishly.

"Uh-oh. It's been more than thirty years since the last one. Maybe I can stand one sermon every thirty years."

"Good. If thirty years is the time span, this will be the last one, I promise. Now, to get back to the story, here I am floating outside my room. The next thing I know I'm traveling along a long, dark tunnel. As I move through the tunnel, I encounter a depth of love, compassion, and peace that is totally unique to my experience. Then the floating stops, and a gentle voice takes me through a life review that begins with my earliest memories. This is judgment, Brenda, but it is so different from what is described in the New Testament. All my failings are examined with a kindness and understanding that brought tears to my eyes.

"When the life review ends, I float further along the tunnel. Upon navigating a sharp bend, I see a light at the end which is blinding in its brilliance. Again, my movement stops. My heart is overflowing with love and the essential goodness of life. As I try to form words to express my gratitude, a voice intrudes which explains I cannot proceed further, that I must return to my body because there is more that I need to do with my life. The next thing I know I am back inside my body, there are several people working around me, and then the tension in the room eases when it is announced they have a heartbeat."

"That is an amazing story."

"It changed my life. It is a journey that millions have taken before me. Psychologists have interviewed literally thousands of people who, like me, came back. Though not absolutely identical, the accounts are essentially the same, the same for atheists and saints, Muslims and Christians, criminals and average blokes like me. While in that tunnel, I did not meet Jesus, nor was I lectured on religious dogma, creeds, or ethical systems. Instead, I encountered love, deep, pure, transforming love."

"Wow," that was initially all that I could say. And then I added, "Explain to me the part that relates to Mom."

"The life review. I was led through my marriage and was able to see so many things in a different light. One of the problems with our relationship I tried to discuss with you many years ago was that your mother was frigid. What I came to understand was that much of her response was due to me. Yes, she inherited some crazy, rather unhealthy, attitudes about sex from her parents, but it was my moodiness and lack of emotional support that made the problem so much worse. Your mother would have been fine if I had been more nurturing, if I had been able to focus on her needs rather than my own."

"Did you ever tell her this?" I asked as tears spilled out all over my face. I turned away from Daddy so that he would not notice. I'm afraid the tone of my voice gave it away.

"No. It was both too difficult and too late. But the near death experience did inspire me to heal our relationship. You can tell her if you want after I'm gone."

"Have you ever tried to explain the experience? Where does all that love come from? Is it God?"

"It's mystery, Sweetheart. There is no final explanation that is totally convincing to me. Science has examined the matter with answers that make some sense. Most of them claim it's a chemical response to a dying brain. But I traveled along that tunnel. I really believed I was on a journey to another world. That's one of the reasons why I don't dread reaching the top of the hill and looking into the other side because then I will know.

"But there is a minimum answer to your question. The near death experience shows us that love has been built into the created universe. This love is abundant. It is worth getting up every morning to affirm it no matter what your situation or condition, and for this love I am deeply grateful. I thank God for it."

"Fantastic, Daddy. Now, listen. I see from my watch that it is 3:45 p.m., and Abby gave me specific instructions about a nap."

"I'm probably too wound up for sleep, but it is a little chilly. Maybe you should put me back in bed, and I can pretend."

"I like that idea. Then Abby will trust me with you again."

"I promise we won't talk about religion."

"I asked for it, Daddy. You only did as you were told," I said as I rose from the chair to take him and the wheelchair inside. I wasn't exactly sure how I would get him from the wheelchair into bed, but I was confident he would have an answer. He had been providing me with answers all of my life.

* * *

I stimulate Daddy. That was how Abby so nicely greeted me the next morning as the two of us shared a cup of coffee outside on their porch. The next six days were one Thanksgiving reunion after another—great food and pleasant gatherings in different settings around their home. Daddy was an enthusiastic participant. He was enjoying himself immensely and wasn't in any pain that I was aware of, although I'm sure he looked on his confinement as a prison sentence. At least that was how I viewed it. The wonderful thing was that if I closed my eyes and just listened, it was as if nothing had changed. That all ended the following Saturday, the day that Mom got here and Ana arrived from Chicago, when Daddy had his final setback. He declined precipitously after that and died Monday morning in his sleep.

There was one other occasion during this period that I want to describe for you. It was largely routine, in many respects not at all out of the ordinary, but it still looms large in my life. It involved Daddy's dinner on

Wednesday night. Abby generally served him his dinner in the late afternoon. It was the one part of his regime that she insisted on doing herself.

We started that afternoon a little after 5 p.m. It usually took an hour or more to complete the task. I was out on the deck talking with Daddy when Abby called out that his dinner was ready. I wheeled him into their first-floor bedroom, and then helped Abby lift him onto the bed. While I propped him up behind pillows and adjusted the plastic oxygen dispenser under his nose, Abby returned to the kitchen for his tray. His evening meal consisted of chicken breast, mashed potatoes, creamed spinach, and Ben and Jerry's ice cream. The last item on the menu never changed.

Abby sat on his bed and assisted with the feeding. She cut the chicken breast into tiny pieces and occasionally helped guide the fork when his shaking right hand needed steadying. There was a cloth napkin on the bed beside the tray to wipe Daddy's mouth when the fork went a little awry, missing its target. I was impressed with Abby's patience. She allowed Daddy to struggle on his own, intervening only when he reached some unbridgeable impasse.

As Abby began her work, I retreated to a chair at the far end of the room and, for the most part, became a silent observer. I winced a little when he used two shaking hands to raise a glass of grapefruit juice to his lips. It was striking how his once rather stumpy hands now looked as if they belonged to a piano player—long and thin, well thin anyway. I smiled at the thought that my father's hair, cut relatively short for all of his life and meticulously held in place, looked like it needed to be cut. The plastic oxygen cord, wrapped around each ear, fluffed out his thinning gray hair in a way that made it look unkept and longer than it actually was. Though gaunt, it had always been, his face was virtually wrinkle free. His look was gentle and refined, intent on what he was doing, though quick to smile when the unintended, though inevitable, fumble took place.

The meal could have been boring and grim, but Daddy's slow, deliberate pace was sprinkled with thoughtful conversation, knowing winks, and moments of laughter. I am sure this is why Abby insisted on performing this task. During one particularly long pause, Daddy looked down at her and said. "You often remind me of my mother, Sweetheart."

"Why is that?" Abby responded.

"You never met her, did you?"

"No, she died five years before we became an item."

"You both took such good care of me," and then, after smiling broadly at her, he raised a spoon of ice cream to his mouth. Tonight it was "Chunky Monkey," one of his many favorites. Ten minutes later he allowed his head to sink into the pillow, and he shut his eyes.

"Are you tired, Jeff?" Abby asked as she gently wiped away the ice cream around his mouth. After a considerable pause, Daddy quietly responded, eyes still closed.

"No, I'm indulging in a little fantasy."

"That's nice, dear. English professors approve of fantasy," she said as she moved a chair right next to the bed, sat down in it, and took his hand. She allowed him some time and then whispered up at him. "Is it nice fantasy?"

With eyes that remained closed, he mumbled. "I'm thinking about a rhododendron canopy along a narrow mountain trail with a broad river, the name of which always escapes me."

"And a pileated woodpecker in the nearby thicket," Abby softly responded.

"I love you, Abby. That was the first time."

"Watching that hawk circle the old fire tower, and you with your arms around me, that is what did me in," she quietly responded as she raised his hand to kiss it. I sat there, silent and forgotten, with tears streaming down my face and a heart that was so full it was ready to burst. As they quietly relived those sacred memories, love infused their bedroom. I felt like an intruder, and yet I was meant to be there. It was Daddy's last lesson, his final and best sermon. As I sat there silently watching, the love between them radiated outward, you could feel it, almost touch it, and my mind was taken to another place. I closed my eyes too; and, as the deep love in that room took over my awareness, I became a Christian.

* * *

I really should end the story here on this emotional high note, but I need to speak briefly about Daddy's memorial service at Holy Cross. It was presided over by the Rt. Reverend Greg Williamson, the retired bishop from western North Carolina. As you can imagine on the afternoon of his memorial celebration, the church was packed—standing room only. Greg entered from the side and walked the short distance to the center of the church just in front of the altar in an open sports jacket, no formal robes, and smiled at those in attendance.

"Welcome to Holy Cross and to the memorial service of one of my oldest friends, Jeff Peterson. It's the job of ministers to preside over formal occasions like marriages and funerals. Twenty-eight years ago the wedding of Abby and Jeff was anything but formal. They got married at the Park alongside the bank of the Watauga River. There were five of us there.

"When Abby took her vows, at one point she promised to grow old with Jeff because she didn't want anyone else to see her wrinkles. Well, if you look at her today, that's a promise she didn't need to make. With the exception of a few gray hairs, she's as beautiful today as that day in October twenty-eight years ago.

"In the spirit of that wedding, today I'm asked to preside over a "Hootin Annie." As you can see, up here with me is Ken Cooper on the guitar and Amy Mast on the keyboard. We will sing ten of Jeff's songs selected by his daughter Brenda. You should have received several sheets of paper stapled together containing the words of the songs as a bulletin insert. Several friends will come forward to introduce each song. Ms. Brenda," and I left my seat in the first pew and stepped to the front of the church.

"Thank you all so much for coming," I said while smiling and fighting back tears. "The first song is entitled "My Friend Jacob." Jacob was a member of my high school class in Concord, Massachusetts. We didn't know much about homosexuality back then, but Jacob was clearly gay and he stood out. Because he was different, he was bullied. "My Friend Jacob" is a song about people who are different and bullied as a result. Daddy always taught me that Jesus was radically inclusive. This song so beautifully expresses that theme. Please stand." After finishing, I turned, smiled at Ken and Amy, the music started, and I returned to my seat.

Eight songs followed in similar fashion on themes ranging from economic justice, racial harmony, world peace, environmental health, the beauty of the universe, and, of course, the beauty of human love. The last song was introduced by Abby. When she reached center stage and turned to face the audience, she had a big smile on her face. I couldn't help but admire her courage.

"When Greg introduced this celebration of Jeff's life, he mentioned one of my wedding vows taken so many years ago. On that day I also promised Jeff I wouldn't be silly, but only on even days. Well, as I'm sure you all are aware, today is October 11th. Now I'm not going to stand up here and be silly even though that ancient contract gives me the right to do so.

I would, however, like to tell you a silly story which I think tells you a lot about Jeff.

"Twenty years ago, maybe it was even further back than that. It's hard to keep track of dates. Time seems to be passing so quickly. Anyway, way back when, Jeff and I were in Porto, the port city in Portugal at the mouth of the Douro River. It was our third gig on the Sea Cloud, and we had the afternoon off. It was the middle of July, hot, and I wanted to go sailing in the beautiful harbor there. I had grown up sailing on Lake Minnetonka in Minnesota. Jeff was quite clueless about the whole thing, although he was a good swimmer which became important as you will soon see.

"We rented a fourteen-foot sailfish and were off. The wind was brisk, coming from the east as I remember, and we were sailing on a broad reach with me at the tiller. All of a sudden this hairbrained idea popped into my head. I hope it was on an odd numbered day on the calendar, but I can't be sure all these years later. Anyway, I let the tiller go free and with both hands yanked in the sail. Of course, we capsized. That was the point.

"Jesus, Abby," Jeff said as he emerged on the surface, treading water. "What the hell are you doing?"

"I'm glad you mentioned Jesus, Jeff," I responded laughing. "This is all about him."

"You've got to be kidding me," Jeff replied as he swam around the bow toward where I was treading water near the stern.

"I need to be baptized Jeff. I'm a sinner. I desperately need forgiveness."

"Jesus may forgive you, but I'm not so sure about me."

"He's far more important Jeffie. Come here quickly and get with it so we can right the boat and be on our way." He swam over to me, placed his hands on my shoulders, and shoved me under. When I came back up, he smiled at me and said:

"I baptize you in the name of the Holy Ghost."

"What happened to Father and Son?"

"The God I know has no masculine identity." I have trained him well I thought, but I kept this thought to myself. "I should also point out that Jesus was a first century Palestinian Jew, a human being, not God's divine son. Ghost is all we have. It will have to do."

"Will this baptism stick? It sounds a little sketchy to me."

"Your biggest problem is that it was performed by a defrocked priest." And he swam two strokes to close the gap between us, put his arms around me, and tried to kiss me as the two of us sank down into the water struggling not to drown. When we emerged at the surface, he smiled at me and said:

"Great time for a swim, Sweetheart. Best way I know to beat this heat. Now my captain, what's our next move?"

"Just grab onto the gunnel and lift yourself onto the keel. She'll come right up. Watch your head, though. The boom may come flying across the boat." Jeff did as he was told, and we arrived back at the rental dock well within the time limit.

"This little incident tells you a lot about Jeff's religion. It comes out even in the strangest of circumstances. It was all about a God of loving spirit. You could have the Trinity as far as Jeff was concerned. This incident also tells you something about our relationship. His initial frustration with me quickly ended in hugs and kisses even if he didn't actually land that kiss in the water. At that wedding ceremony when Greg asked if I would promise to obey I answered with fingers crossed. With Jeff such protective measures were not necessary. I never needed to cross my fingers," and she turned from the audience and burst into tears.

After regaining her composure, she turned back toward the audience to announce the last song. "We will end this afternoon with "Peace Begins With Me." After the song, don't forget the reception in the Apple Barn, and thank you all so much for coming. To many of you a special thanks for all you have done for our family over the last month.

"This song is certainly not our best, but it's my favorite because it's our first. We wrote it together before we were married at the house during a two-day rainstorm. It was my first trip to Beaver Dam, a trip I made myself in heavy rain from Blowing Rock following Jeff. It was a trip I will never forget. The roads have not improved much since that day.

"You will note we omitted the chorus from your music sheets. That was done deliberately. To begin with, the lyric is not very good. But most important, I want you to focus on the guitar solo. That was Jeff at his best." She turned away from the audience to say: "Take it away Ken and Amy. It was your music that made this celebration so special." She then made her way back to her seat on the first pew.

Following the song, Greg stepped forward for the benediction. "Thank you LORD for giving us Jeffrey Peterson whose life was such a beautiful expression of your loving presence. His being simply radiated it. In remembrance of my great friend and in the name of the Holy Ghost, I say Amen."

Appendix

Biblical Passages Pertaining to The Salvation Myth

1. For Jesus's view that the kingdom of God was imminent, within the lifetime of his followers, see Mark 1:15 and 9:1, Matthew 3:2 and 10:7 and Luke 9:27.

2. For Daniel's prophecy of the Son of Man, see Daniel 7: 13-14.

3. For Stephen's vision of Jesus as the Son of Man, see Acts 7: 56.

4. For passages citing the imminent return of the Son of Man, within the first century, see Mark 13: 26-31, Matthew 24: 30-34, and Luke 21: 27-32.

5. For contrasting views of where the physical resurrection of Jesus took place, see Matthew 28: 16-20 and Luke 24: 33-43.

6. For a discussion of Paul's account of Jesus's resurrection as a vision experience, see Acts 9: 1-9 and Acts 26: 12-17. Pay special attention to Acts 26: 16 where Paul specifically states that his encounter with the resurrected Jesus was a vision experience.

7. For Paul's claim that flesh and blood do not inherit the kingdom of God, see 1 Corinthians 15: 42-44.

8. For Paul's claim that his encounter with the resurrected Jesus was the same as that of the disciples, see 1 Corinthians 15: 4-8.